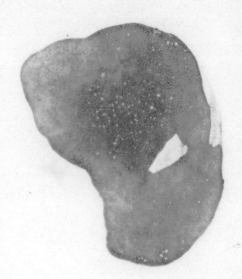

GOOD GIRLS DON'T GET MURDERED

f
PAR

M

Good Girls Don't Get Murdered

Percy Spurlark Parker

CHARLES SCRIBNER'S SONS
New York

This book published simultaneously in the
United States of America and in Canada—
Copyright under the Berne Convention

1 3 5 7 9 11 13 15 17 19 V/C 20 18 16 14 12 10 8 6 4 2

Printed in the United States of America
Library of Congress Catalog Card Number 74-14008
ISBN 0-684-13907-3

To Shirley
  My part-time secretary, my full-time wife

GOOD GIRLS DON'T GET MURDERED

1

Big Bull Benson crushed the nub of a cigar out in the ash tray that was kept behind the bar. There were only two people in the lounge he had not seen before, the dude sleeping at a back table, and the broad at the end of the bar. Normally he did not allow anyone to sleep in his place, but it was Monday, a slow night. There were only five other customers in the joint, three regulars who sat at the bar across from the TV set, rapping and digging an old Bogart movie, plus Harry and his old lady who sat at one of the booths.

He was working the bar tonight because Sam Devlin had called in sick. It meant missing the poker game at Skinny Joe's but he did not mind. He had dropped over a grand at the last two games. Maybe breaking the cycle would change his luck.

The broad at the end of the bar tapped her glass on the counter top, and he grabbed the bottle of J&B. It would be her seventh drink in a little under three hours, and it had not seemed to phase her at all. She just sat there, smoking and drinking her Scotch on the rocks, not bothering anyone. Sugar Carl had made a play for her, and split when he saw there was no action to be had.

He rinsed her glass, added a couple of ice cubes, studying her closer as he poured the drink. She was a notch better than average. Her skin was a smooth dark brown. Her natural hairdo was not curly, but a high thick bush that was peaked at her forehead. She wore no make-up except on her arched eyebrows and lashes. The gold hoop of a dog collar matched her earrings. She was slender, yet, unless the bra was padded, well equipped.

"Just how much of that stuff can you suck up?" he asked, as she raised her glass.

She swallowed, sat the glass down without looking at him. "You're getting paid for it, why worry?"

"Hell, baby, I ain't worrying, just curious. Usually there's only a couple of reasons a woman comes in a bar alone. She's waiting for somebody, or she's working. You don't seem to be doing either."

She shrugged, puffed on her cigarette. Smoke filled the air between them, dispensed in various spiraling patterns. "I've got some heavy thinking to do, mister. I don't need any help."

"Trouble, huh?" That was one of the oldest reasons people drank.

She looked at him, her eyes a mite red, her words harsh.

"I didn't read any signs outside calling this a church, and you don't look like any damn priest to me."

"Cool it, baby," he said, holding his hand up. "I don't mean to get nosey. I'm Bull Benson. I own this place and the hotel, too, for that matter," he said, not being boastful, but in an effort to explain himself. "I'm trying to say that you look like you need help. Maybe, now just maybe, I can offer it to you."

He had tried different tacks on various women. He did not have any real trouble in finding a bed partner. He neither went after all he saw, nor accepted all that he could get. The strange thing here was after he made his offer, he realized he meant it. There was something about her, something about her sitting there, drinking in solitude. It was a loud cry for help.

"Just drop it, huh. I think better alone."

He shrugged. "The offer's still there," he said, wanting to say more but deciding not to, and walked back to the Bogart-watching threesome at the bar.

"Hit us again, Bull, and we'll split," Ralph said. He was sitting in the middle—a dude of medium dark complexion, with such a thick and unruly mustache that he actually had to part and brush it aside before drinking.

"That Bogart was a tough bastard."

3

He poured up three beers, sitting the mugs in front of them.

"Yeah, sure was," Will nodded, a thin little stud who made a trip to the toilet every fifteen minutes once he started drinking heavily. His inability to hold his piss was a common joke around the place. Bets were placed on just how many times he would go.

Harry called to him, pointed to the money he left on the table, and he and his old lady left. There was really no reason to stay open any longer. He flipped the TV off in the middle of a rabbi conducting a sermonette. He picked up the intercom, buzzed the kitchen and told Ed to start locking the joint up, they would be closing early.

He went down to the end of the bar, poured her another J&B. "This one's on me," he said. "I'm apologizing."

She looked from him to the Scotch, then back. With a slight smile she nodded, raised the glass in a toast to him, and drank. "Maybe, I should apologize myself," she said, replacing the glass on the counter.

"No need," he told her. "When I'm into some heavy thinking myself, I don't dig being bothered."

She smiled again, a broader smile this time, exposing even white teeth. It seemed the longer he looked at her, the more he found that he liked.

"New in the neighborhood, or do you just do your thinking in different parts of town?"

"New," she said. "I just moved into the Lairmont this morning."

"The Lairmont, that dump! I've got better rooms here and cheaper too!" He started to laugh. "Excuse the sales pitch, it pops out every now and then."

She smiled with him.

"Say, look. Since you live so close, it'd be silly to offer you a ride, but I'd be glad to walk you there. That's if you don't mind."

She toyed with the drink, looked up at him, her eyes somewhat redder now, a mite glassy, the effects of the liquor beginning to show. He wondered just how much hold the Scotch had on her. He had known people who could sit and pour the booze down, and no one could tell it until they stood and tried to walk.

She nodded. "Thanks, I'd like that."

"Mellow," he said, patting her on her hand. "Hold tight until I clear this place out."

The only entrance or exit from behind the bar was a small swinging gate right next to where she sat. He used it, going first to the booth where Harry had sat, getting the money he left there. Next, to the joker sleeping at the back table.

"Okay, brother, time to go home," he said, shaking him on his shoulder.

The dude stirred, bumping into the near empty mug of beer he had bought when he first came into the joint, a little after the broad had showed. He sat up looking about the place. His hair was a brownish tangle about his head. His beard seemed more the result of a lack of shaving rather than of an honest attempt to grow one. It grew in uneven patches about his face, giving the silhouette of his

5

face a lumpy appearance. His right ear lobe was pierced, not the most common practice around, and yet not uncommon. "What's the matter?"

"I'm closing, brother. Got to find some place else to cop your Z's."

"Yeah, sure," the dude said, standing. He was wearing a black lightweight jacket. He zipped it all the way up, mumbled a goodnight, and walked crookedly toward the door.

"We're going to make it too, Bull," Ralph said, sliding off the bar stool.

"Take it slow, fellows," he told them. "Thanks for coming by."

He locked the door behind them, went back to the bar.

"You haven't told me your name."

"Is that the fee for walking me home?"

He smiled. "Not one cent less."

She hesitated. "Alicia," she said, finally.

It was a nice name. He liked it. He could not recall personally knowing anyone by that name—if it was her name.

Ed Lambert, the cook, came through the swinging doors which gave access to the washrooms, the office, and the kitchen. He had not gone along with the Afro, but kept his hair processed, slick and shiny, parted in the middle. The two men weighed nearly the same, but he was a full head taller than Ed. Most of Ed's weight was in the gut, which hung over his belt like an over-inflated balloon. Someone was always asking Ed about going on a diet. He would tell them that it was bad business for a cook to be skinny, people would think he did not enjoy his own cooking.

"Handle things here, Ed," he said, reaching behind the bar for his suit coat. "I'm going to take the lady home."

"Maybe I ought ta start tending bar," Ed said. "I never get ta meet any good looking chicks back in that kitchen."

He slipped his coat on. Standing, she took her purse off the counter, a dark green leather bag that matched her shoes. He helped her into the jacket of her pants suit. He got a whiff of perfume, light, sweet, not an over-indulgence in some exotic fragrance. He liked that. Her green bell-bottom outfit did not hug her hips too tightly, yet enough to show what was there. He liked the look it presented. He also liked the fact that she was taller than he first noticed. Six feet six himself, he was partial to taller women.

"You said you own all this," she asked, once outside.

"Yeah," he replied, looking back at the six-story structure, its rows of shaded windows.

It had rained earlier, but the night was warm against his face. The scent of barbecued ribs came to him from the rib joint down the street. The street was quiet, except for the distant cry of a baby.

His building sat in the middle of the block. The sign hanging over the entrance read: "Benson Hotel, Transients Welcome." The restaurant-lounge took up most of the first floor. The glowing, red neon strip across the expanse of the window proclaimed it to be THE BULLPEN.

He was raised in this neighborhood, and had seen the hotel most of his life. He had played about it as a kid; been its patron. He had never thought of owning the joint. The idea of a whore house was somewhere back in his mind, but never a fifty-room transient hotel.

"I always wish I can tell folks I did it with hard work and saving my money. Hell, truth is I won the deed in a poker game about five years ago."

He said it lightly, but the deed had been acquired in a thirty-six hour set. The last five hours had been a two-handed cutthroat duel between him and the former owner, Willie Longtree. The papers had been signed over to him, and Longtree had not been seen in the neighborhood since. Some said he had gone to L.A. and got offed in a crooked crap game. Others said he had taken up missionary work in South America.

"Thinking now, seems I've heard of you," she said, as they started walking towards the Lairmont, which was on the corner of the next block.

"I get mentioned around," he said.

She looped her arm about his, but not for support. She was in control of the Scotch.

"Five, six months ago, weren't you in the paper for something?"

He nodded. "It was closer to eight months. I helped a friend out of a murder rap. I'll tell you about it some day."

She tugged gently on his arm, smiling up at him. Her eyes seemed to sparkle, or maybe it was just the reflection of the street lamp. "Promise?" she asked.

"Sure."

Her change of moods confused him somewhat,

from her harshness at the lounge to her apparent flirtatiousness now. Trouble does not go away that fast. People try to hide it, to forget it, but it is still there.

He wanted to ask her what had been bothering her. But, maybe he was simply making too much of it. Maybe it was just a quarrel she had had with her main dude.

He wondered if Alicia was her real name.

He saw the phone booth near the corner, its light out, but he could see the darkened figure of some-one inside. He was cautious as they approached it. On the streets of a neighborhood like his, self de-fense is the first thing that is learned. He was a big man, but he knew there were dudes hungry enough to try him. She was talking but he was not aware of what she was saying. They passed the booth and he looked back, seeing a partial silhou-ette of a bearded face.

She tugged at his arm again. He turned back to her. "You realize I propositioned you. You didn't even answer me?"

He laughed, told her he was sorry, and started to explain about the phone booth, when he heard its door open. He was swinging back towards the booth when he heard the shot, felt pain roar through his head in waves. Brilliant flashes of light changed into a whirling darkness as he began to fall.

CHAPTER

A woman's scream, high shrilled.

Footsteps running, getting louder.

Someone shouting for the police.

His head seemed to vibrate with each throb as he opened his eyes to try to orientate himself. The sidewalk was cool and dry to his cheek, and there was a line of something red and shiny before him. Alicia. He raised partially, the throbbing increasing. A haze seemed to float through his vision. She lay face down on the sidewalk. A triangle of three dark blotches grew on the back of her jacket, gaining red overtones. Blood flowed from her in several different streams, angling with the cracks in the sidewalk out onto the street. He called to her, tried to stand. The throbbing became louder, the haze returned darker.

It was the harsh scent of ammonia that brought him out of it the second time. He pushed the hand holding the smelling salts away, as his eyes focused on the white cop bending over him. He was young and obviously had grown a mustache to make himself look older, but it did not seem to go with his small boyish face.

"Bull, you okay?" Ed Lambert stood next to the cop, his face sweaty.

"Sure he is," the cop said. His name plate, which hung on the flap of his right shirt pocket read: D. F. RYAN. "Come on, give me a hand," Ryan said. "We'll get him over to my squadrol and take care of that wound."

"Wound?" He touched his temple, just to the right of his forehead. It was the spot where the pain was greatest. It felt damp and warm. Looking at the thin film of blood on his fingertips, he realized how close he had come to being killed.

They helped him to his feet. The sidewalk seemed to tilt under him. His head felt like someone was striking him with a hammer. Ed held his arm tighter, steadying him. He nodded him a thanks.

"Alicia," he said. "What about—"

Someone had thrown a blanket over her, one foot protruded, her thick-heeled shoe partially off. Blood stained the blanket in two different places. Whatever her troubles had been, they were certainly over now. If only he had been more cautious when they approached the phone booth! If only he had turned sooner. But what would he have been able to do?

There was a crowd on both sides of him, uniformed cops holding them back, black faces peering over and around, trying to learn what had happened. He recognized Little Man Ray, Hustlin' Freddie, and Sam Conley, and thought he heard his name among their rumble. Two patrol cars were at the curb, their dome lights throwing blue flashes throughout the scene. The light traveled over him, the crowd, to the buildings across the street where people stood at their windows digging the night's main event.

They got him to the back seat of the first patrol car. Ryan took a first-aid kit from the glove compartment and started working on his forehead.

"What happened?" Ryan asked.

"I don't know, some dude just started throwing lead at us."

"Thirty-eight automatic at close range. There's some spent shells by the phone booth."

"Damn, Bull," Ed said. "Who done it?"

"That last dude that was in the joint, I think, but I really didn't get a good look. We walked past the phone booth, and bang."

Ryan was tearing the sanitized paper off a bandage when he stopped and looked at him, his small green eyes intent. "You said the suspect was in your place?"

"I told ya," Ed interrupted. "He owns the hotel and lounge down the street."

"I know, I know," said Ryan. "I've been hearing about Bull Benson ever since I started on this beat. But what about the suspect?"

He told him about the bearded dude who had been sleeping at a back table, and of seeing someone in the phone booth who resembled him. "But I'm not sure," he said. The throbbing in his head was still present.

"That's okay," Ryan said, as he finished stripping the bandage, and placed it on his wound. "You just sit here. I'll grab one of the lab boys, and your man and I'll go down and check out the table where the suspect sat. We might turn up some prints."

"Damnit to hell," Ed said, slapping the side of his face. "I'd already cleaned the table and the glass the guy used before I heard the first siren."

Ryan's mouth was pushed out somewhat under the shabby mustache. He sighed. "Well, we'll take a look anyway."

They left him sitting in the patrol car, left him to the noise and staring of the crowd, left him to the throbbing which took on vigor in his solitude, left him with the thought of Alicia's gentle tug on his arm.

Two white guys were taking pictures of her now. One was holding the blanket back, while the other got several shots at different angles. It takes a hell of a long time for the dead in a murder case to get their rest. The lab dudes with their cameras, the autopsy later, sometimes the sanctity of the grave is broken.

He saw Vern Wonler and Charlie Evans parking

13

their unmarked car across the street. The two men, a Detective Sergeant and a Detective, pushed their way through the crowd going over to the dude with the camera. Vern was tall, lean. Charlie beefy, thick chested.

He turned away from them, leaning back onto his seat with his eyes closed, the throbbing, still the throbbing. Nausea came upon him, and he swallowed hard to contain himself.

The high-pitched whine of a police siren blared in the distance, got louder as the vehicle approached. But he did not look to see what it was. Probably the paddy wagon coming for the body. It was due. He did not open his eyes until he heard the doors to the patrol car open. He slid over as Vern climbed in back with him. Charlie sat up front.

"Shit's flying again, huh, baby?" Vern said, nodding his long narrow head. A thin line of a mustache grew under his flat nose. His natural hairdo was moderate in length, not as close as he once wore it, not quite as bushy as the style had become.

He had known Vern for over twenty years. They had grown up together. Mugging, gambling, running for the numbers men, there was not much they had not done. At one time they actually began to organize the neighborhood, to have their own black mafia.

Vern was a year older than him, and had gotten in on the last months of Korea. When his enlistment was up, he had returned home with a different outlook. "The streets ain't where it's at for me anymore," Vern had told him back then. "I need something solid, something to build on." He had taken the police exam shortly after.

He returned Vern's greeting, speaking to Charlie also, but got no reply. He neither expected one nor gave a damn for not getting it. Charlie was a thick-lipped bastard, clean shaven, his hair cut close to his scalp, with eyes that always seemed too small for his puffy-jowled square-chin face. He was a black cop from the old school, who jumped on his own kind harder than anyone else. He hated crime and criminals with an intensity that was close to passion. And if the criminal was black that intensity became a near rage.

He wondered why Charlie had not been hauled off the force years ago. Then he thought, hell, he was only committing mayhem on black folks. Vern had once said, "Sure he's rough, and I don't really dig his methods. But out there in the streets, when I've got to bust into a room, or go into a dark alley, there's nobody I'd rather have backing me."

He dug into his pocket for a cigar, hoping a smoke would help ease the queasiness within him. The cigar was smashed and broken in three places. He tossed it to the floor of the patrol car, and Vern handed him a cigarette. Vern lit it for him, then took one for himself. Charlie did not smoke.

The taste of a cigarette was not as satisfying as a cigar would have been. The smoke was lighter. He was careful to hold the cigarette between his lips and not with his teeth as he would have done a cigar. It was awkward, but better than no smoke at all.

"Want to run it down to us, Bull?" Vern asked.

He nodded, and started his story. He really did

15

not have much to tell, repeating the story he had told Ryan. This time he went over it slower, trying not to leave anything out. But his head was hurting so badly that he was not sure just what he was saying.

"Let's go over that description again, Benson," Charlie said, glancing at the note pad he had been writing in. "Light-skinned negro, early twenties, bearded, reddish brown hair, five-eight or nine, 'bout a hundred and fifty pounds, wearing dark slacks and a black jacket. Is that it? No identifying marks, no other details?"

"That's all, Charlie. That's all I can think of, anyway. And as I said, I ain't sure he was the stud in the phone booth. It happened too fast."

Charlie nodded, his big lips in a frown. "I bet half the scum out there saw the deal go down," he said, indicating the crowd with another nod. "Your buddies, huh, Benson? Not one of 'em showed ta give ya a hand."

He did not feel like arguing the ethics of the street with Charlie. He knew that as far as most of the folks were concerned, as black as Charlie was, he was still the whitest cop on the force.

"What about the broad?" Charlie asked. "Still saying you don't know her?"

"We met tonight, I was walking her to her hotel."

"I'm suppose ta believe that jive, Benson? Hell, she was your kind of woman. Good girls don't get murdered."

"Get laid," he said, his head throbbing in sharper pain, the urge to swing on Charlie beginning to grow.

16

"Cool it, both of you," Vern said.

"Sure, and let that ace of yours lie." Charlie said.

"I don't believe he's lying."

"Beautiful," Charlie said, his lips in a frown.

There was silence for a moment, then Vern said, "Alicia's the babe's name all right. We checked her purse. Alicia Hill. Social security, few credit cards, key to a room at the Lairmont, but nothing on any permanent address. Running it down shouldn't be too hard, though."

She had told him the truth about her name, but what did that mean? Would she have told him about her troubles? Would she have expected his help? His head pained too much for him to concentrate.

"At least we can be sure he was after the woman," Vern said. "With as many slugs as he put in her. If you want to look at it this way, you can be lucky that first slug just grazed you. Otherwise, you might be laying out there with a blanket over you too."

"Luck of the Irish," he said, not feeling very lucky. A gambler made his luck by knowing the games well, the odds. He learned to read the people, dig where they were coming from. He could tell if the cards or the dice were straight, and if they were not he knew what to do about it. He could ride the tempo of a game and knew when some sucker was ripe for the picking. Luck, hell. Luck did not have a damn thing to do with it. It had been close, but luck did not have a thing to do with him not being blown away tonight. It simply was not his time.

The cigarette began to burn his finger. He realized he had just been sitting there holding it in his lap. There was enough left for one last puff. He took it, a deep drag, holding the smoke in his lungs a long time before expelling it. It helped some, helped to ease the pounding in his head, but not much. He dropped the butt to the floor stepping on it as Ryan and Ed came up to the patrol car.

Vern rolled the window down. "Come up with anything, Ryan?"

"No, Sir," Ryan said. "Mr. Lambert, here, had cleaned the table and glass the suspect used. The fingerprint boys drew blanks."

Ed shrugged, his big black face somber, his eyes partially closed. "Damn, man, I feel like an ass. I mean we might have a lead on the dude if I hadn't—"

"Forget it, Ed," Vern said. "We can't blame you for doin' your job."

"Yeah, but I still don't feel right about it. Say, Bull, you don't look too cool, man."

He had began to weave somewhat in his seat. The throbbing was more steady now.

"He's right, you don't look too good," Vern added.

"I'll admit I don't feel like running Main," he said. He was referring to the time when he and Vern were kids. Back then, the toughest teen gang in the neighborhood was the Main Street Busters. They claimed the eight hundred block of Main as theirs, and used an old store front as their head-quarters. It was a test to see how much balls a dude had if he would run that block on Main. He and Vern had done it often.

Vern grinned. As always his teeth were tobacco stained. "Well, I think I could make it, but I haven't had a .38 slug bounce off my skull. We better get you to the hospital. You could have a concussion. Just make sure you get over to the precinct tomorrow so we can get a statement."

"We ought ta take him to the precinct now," Charlie said. "Ain't nothing wrong with that hard-headed bastard."

"Thanks, Charlie baby," he said. "I love you too."

He stayed in Ryan's patrol car, and it was used to transport him the six blocks to Jayburn Community Hospital.

He knew some of the doctors there, and a great many more of the nurses. He got a lot of their trade at his place, both the lounge and the hotel.

Dr. Matthew James was on duty in the emergency room when he came in. Doc Matt, as most of the people in the neighborhood called him, was a gray-haired old guy who played poker like a pro, and more than once had out-drunk him.

The Doc took him through a hour of X-rays and various tests. There was no fracture, Doc Matt finally assured him, and added that he would feel better after a night's rest. The Doc admitted him to a room, gave him a sedative, and bid him goodnight.

The sedative worked fast, but not fast enough to keep the picture of Alicia out of his mind. He went to sleep with images of her dancing about him, all bloody and dead.

CHAPTER

3

There were no visions of Alicia as he slept, and he awakened rested. His headache was gone. His body seemed light, relaxed. It was as if the solid sleep of the sedative had rejuvenated him, giving him a jolt of new life.

LIFE.

What did Alicia have now—a slab in the morgue. It came upon him then, the whole of what had happened. Murder. It was not someone being killed in a robbery, or someone dying in an accident. Premeditated murder, planned, executed. Why? Why Alicia?

Charlie had said it. Good girls don't get murdered. Whatever it was, whatever her troubles had been, she was playing in a high stakes game. People don't take a hand in a deal like that blindly. Definitely she would not be a candidate for any citizenship award. Or was he just trying to convince himself to stay out of it?

He checked out of the hospital at noon, grabbing lunch at the hospital cafeteria with a couple of interns he knew. Then he went outside to get a cab to take him to the Moore Street Precinct.

He stood at the curb as the strange mixture of the sun's warmth and the wind's chill played about him. An old Ford pulled up. Forest Westerfield leaned toward him from behind the steering wheel. "Can I give you a lift, Bull?"

"If it's not out of your way, Wes. I've got to run by the Moore Street Precinct."

"Hell, how could it be out of my way, when I've been waiting for you."

"In that case," he said, climbing in. The sweet burnt tobacco scent filled the car, although Wes's pipe sat bowl down in the ash tray.

Wes was a feature writer for the *Daily Challenger*, the newspaper that was circulated primarily in the black communities on the South and West sides of the city. It was a little too graphic for some people, but as Wes had once said, life in the street was graphic.

Wes guided the Ford out into traffic. "I tried to get in to see you, but Doc Matt had given orders that you weren't to have any visitors." He was in his mid-forties, with receding gray-speckled hair, but he managed to be as energetic as any younger guy might be. His thick horn-rimmed glasses were prominent against his tan skin.

Seeing Wes made him realize he had not given any thought to the press—an oversight. There would be questions from them as well as from the police. Cops he could handle. He had been dealing with them most of his life. But the press was something else. He was glad Wes was the first to contact him. He had gotten to know Wes some eight months ago, when he was helping Hal Rodgers out of that murder rap. Rodgers was a hustler, a thief, and a half-assed pimp, but not a murderer. Getting into the case, he had been able to prove it, and Wes had done a story on him. It had him looking like some kind of a black Robin Hood.

"Big Bull Benson rides again," Wes said. "You make good copy. Take a look."

There was a folded *Challenger* on the dashboard. He opened it up to a front page photo of himself, along with a picture of Alicia as she lay on the sidewalk. The two pictures took up half the page.

" 'Course the big rags got you next to the obits. They only go front page if one of their own gets it down here."

"I don't know which I prefer. A man in my business doesn't need publicity."

"Nonsense, Bull, you're one of the few local black celebrities we have. Let us enjoy you."

He laughed. "So enjoy," he said.

There was not much information in the story. Alicia had taken a room at the Lairmont under the name of Jane Brownings late Friday evening. She had spent the weekend in the room, sending out for meals. To the hotel clerk's knowledge, last night had been the first time she left the room. The police had searched her room, but did not disclose whether they had found anything or not. There was a short tag in there about him being slightly injured in the shooting, and at present was not available for questioning. It ended with the usual plea by the police for information which would be held in strict confidence.

"Whatd'you think?" Wes asked, as he gave the car a little more gas, just making the light at Claxson and 64th Street. "Kid named Perry Rawlings did the story. Majoring in journalism at City College, got another year to go."

"He got the address to my place right."

Wes laughed. "The kid'll be damn good one day. Got to learn to dig more, though. He didn't know you were in the hospital. I found that out. And he should have played up the angle about the girl being in hiding."

"He did seem to skim over that."

"Did he skim anything else, Bull?"

There are as many different degrees in trouble as there are combinations that will make a full house. Alicia was in trouble, and because she had been killed for it, any punk could figure it had been serious trouble. But when the fact that she had been hiding was thrown into the pot, that meant she was damn aware of how serious her troubles were.

Just what did this mean to him? Three days she

23

had stayed in hiding. Her first trip out she had come to his bar. She had not tried to leave the city, to lose herself even more. No, she had come to his bar. Why? She had seen the story Wes wrote about him, she mentioned that. Had she actually come to him for help? Naw, he could not believe that, he was reaching too far.

The car rocked as Wes stopped for the light at Eller Street. He pushed his glasses back on his nose. "Aha, Spring. Praise d'Lawd." He nodded towards a gal who turned the corner and started down the street in the direction they had come. Her dress was just a thin line beneath the hem of her mini coat. Her legs were a little heavy, but well shaped.

The light had changed. "I should've dropped you off and grabbed her," Wes said. "Wouldn't mind interviewing her. Bet she's got an interesting story to tell."

"Is that how you do it? I was wondering how an old fart like you made out."

Wes shrugged, grinning. "It doesn't work as well as it used to. Seems more and more to fall back on the power of the dollar."

Another five minutes and they were at the Moore Street Precinct. "Thanks for the ride."

"Forget it, even though you didn't tell me a damn thing."

"The whole story's in the *Challenger,* I didn't see a thing." There had been no mention of the dude with the beard. He still was not sure if he was the same one who had been in the phone booth, but if the cops had not released any info on him, he would not either.

Wes nodded, his lips pushed out. "Bull, ole buddy, the day you don't see what's going on around you is the day the Martians will be down here to castrate us all."

It was silly to try to fox Wes. He had been on the scene too long. "Okay," he said. "When I know something for sure, I'll get back to you."

"Mellow by me, Bull. Catch you later."

The precinct house sat directly across the street from the Mountain Of Eternal Love Tabernacle. That was a one-story brick structure recessed off the walk to allow for a ten-car parking area. The building had always been white, but the name seemed to change with every rain. When he was a kid, in his early teens, it used to be the Holy Manger Baptist Church. His mother hauled his sister, brother, and himself there every Sunday morning, while his old man slept another one off.

He was sixteen when his old man got killed as part of an attempted bank holdup. He could still remember the fuss the brothers and sisters of the church made over him. The hugs, the hand shakes, the pats on his back, telling him he was the man of the family now. Hell, he had been the man in the family for some time. It was his hustling that had brought in most of the food, paid the rent. It had not been easy, but he had learned a lot, learned the ways of the street.

The detective division was on the third and top floor of the precinct. The scene was the same as it had been on his previous visits. Most of the dozen or so desks that spanned the squad room were occupied. There were detectives typing out reports, others interviewing witnesses, victims, and the punks who had made the mistake of getting caught. Some old woman was practically crying onto the shoulder of Amos Tate, a detective. A dude with a rather bored air about himself sat cuffed to the bench against the far wall. It was easy to tell he had been through the bit before, and could lay odds on how much time he would get hit with, and how much he would actually do before he was out again. A fag was sitting at Vic Sawmann's desk, decked out in white boots, black stockings, and a dark brown long-sleeved jersey mini. He probably made a nice looking woman, but someone had altered that. The whole left side of his face was swollen and discolored, and his reddish brown wig sat crookedly upon his head.

He said his hellos on his way to Lou Ruzeales's desk. Lou looked up from his struggle with the typewriter.

"Bull baby, what's happening?" It was more of a greeting than a question.

"Same ole, same ole, Lou. Dropped by to get that statement together for Vern."

"Sure thing," Lou said. He was a wide-faced Puerto Rican whose parents had brought him over when he was about five for a better life in America. Lou, he knew, had wound up fighting the same type of battles then and now that he had done and was doing. "Let me get one of the broads up from the pool," Lou said, standing. "Take room three, I'll send her in."

The stenographer was a prissy little bitch who gave him the impression that if anyone offered her a lay she would faint. She was short and thin and sat straight in her chair as she typed his statement. They sat at opposite ends of a table which was against the wall of the small, dull, gray little room. He tried to recall every detail, Alicia's mood, her effect upon him, the dude with the beard. It did not take long, and he was signing the triplicate copies when Lieutenant Hamilton came into the room.

He always thought that Hamilton's desire was to own a straw hat and a whip, and to make his daily rounds to see to it that his niggers were breaking their asses to get the fields worked. But since those days were somewhat gone, he had settled for being a white cop in a black neighborhood.

It was one of the main reasons Charlie got away with so much shit. Hamilton did not give a damn how many heads got busted, as long as the natives were kept under control.

Hamilton was pot-bellied and balding. The only hair on his head was thick grayish sideburns connected by darker strands above the nape of his neck. Gray, almost white eyebrows over gray eyes gave the face its pastel overtones, drained of any vivid color. His nose was wide and slightly hooked over prominent thick lips. There was nothing he liked about Hamilton, not his looks, not his mannerisms, not one damn thing. He knew Hamilton felt the same about him.

"Are you about finished here, Miss Willis?" Hamilton asked.

"All done, sir," she said. "Mr. Benson was just signing his statement."

"Fine, you can leave us then."

27

"Yes, sir." She closed the door behind her.

Hamilton took the statement off the desk. Reading it, he said, "There's not much more here than what you told Charlie and Vern last night."

"It's as much as I can recall." He knew Hamilton would not let it go at that. He had taken the time to come in here, and it was not just to see how he was feeling.

"It gets closer every time," Hamilton said, sitting on the table where he could look down at him and feel superior probably. "You'll screw up one of these days and I'll have you."

"Sure." He nodded up at him.

Hamilton's eyes seem to grow dark under his white eyebrows. "You want to laugh, don't you? Laugh because I can't do a damn thing to you. Go ahead, get it out of your goddamn system, punk. But don't think I believe any of this shit in this statement." He waved the papers at him.

He did not like things pushed in his face. He felt a flash of heat pass through him. Mentally, he measured the distance from his left hand to the right side of Hamilton's jaw. He could imagine himself swinging, the feel of Hamilton's jaw as his fist made contact, and Hamilton being knocked into the wall under the force of the blow.

It was a pleasant thought, a desirable one. It was just the excuse Hamilton would want.

Hamilton threw the statement back onto the table. He was frowning, his mouth pulled down at its corners. "What was the babe to you, Benson? Why did you set her up? Who did you have do the job?"

"I was just wondering if all the white folks in the

city know what a great job you're doing keeping us poor crime-crazed blacks in line down here?"

The bland face became red, the eyebrows low over his eyes. "Don't bring race into this, Benson. That's the first thing you black bastards yell these days, that somebody's being unfair to you. Color hasn't got anything to do with what's between us. We're talking about murder."

"You're either crazy, or you think I am." He stood, looking down at Hamilton now. "You got my statement. Do what you want with it, I've got nothing to add." He tried to sound as hard and as cold as possible. He wanted to show Hamilton that he had not been impressed one bit. Most of his sessions with the police were a matter of who got their bluff in first.

But the one truth Hamilton told was that it was murder. Alicia's murder. So what if a slug had played ping-pong with his noggin. He had not been the real target. Forgetting the whole thing would be the smart answer.

Hamilton bit at his lower lip, nodded. "Okay, Benson, get going. You're free for now, but I'm not giving up on this. You'll screw up sooner or later."

Screwing up did not bother him, mistakes were made and he simply tried to guard against them. But he felt Hamilton would not hesitate to frame him if the opportunity was there.

"Now, now, Lieutenant, how could I dare do anything wrong, with such a big bad cop like you watching me?"

Hamilton smiled. "Benson, cocky sons of bitches are a pleasure to squash."

CHAPTER

4

He did not stop at the lounge when he got back to the hotel, but checked at the desk to see if there were any messages.

Beth was on duty now. Her gold-trimmed granny glasses sat on the bump that was her nose, and it seemed that she looked over them more than she looked through them.

She had been working for him just under a year now, and he considered her his best employee. Whatever job he laid on her, she handled it exactly as he wanted, without a squabble. He was glad to have her around.

"Jay and Millie called," she told him from

across the counter, "and a couple of women who didn't give their names. They were checking on your health. Didn't ask ta have you call them back, though. You are all right, aren't you?"

"Yeah, sure," he said, touching the small bandage over his right eye. The wound was a little tender. "I'll only have to wear this for a couple of days. If anybody wants me, I'll be upstairs."

He took the elevator, having to punch the sixth floor button twice before the gears took hold, and he remembered that he had meant to have someone take a look at the damn thing a week ago.

A shower, some fresh clothes. Then he would call in his bets for tomorrow's races before digging the action at the lounge. That was his plan. He laid most of his bets with Abe Levinthal who had been running a tailor shop on 60th and Hall for the past twenty years and was the squarest book in the city.

He had given his statement to the cops. He was clear of it now. He was going to stay clear.

His apartment took up the entire south corner of the sixth floor. It was actually three apartments combined to make a spacious six-room flat. Longtree, the former owner, had it fixed up this way for himself. The pad was laid out in such a fashion that the only major change he made in the past five years was the addition of a color TV in the bedroom.

He saw Toni when he came into his apartment, standing by the bar mixing drinks. She had her back to him, but that ass could not be mistaken in a nudist camp. She wore a tan jersey mini that hugged her hips and showed a lot of her long smooth legs. Her slippers were heelless white balls of fur. She wore no stockings and probably no undergarments either. She liked to feel free, she had once said.

She swung around with drinks in hand as he closed the door. "Hi, baby," she said, coming to him. Her long brown hair was done in a pigtail, hanging down over her left shoulder. Her hairdo seemed to make her ears stand out, but it did not spoil the picture. Her eyes were large, brown, clear. Her nose was slender, almost dainty. Her mouth small, yet full-lipped. It was mostly a little girl's face, the eyes giving it an innocent quality, but it was definitely a woman's body.

He took the drink and the kiss that was offered, tasting faintly the strawberry flavor of her lipstick. It did not take much to fix him a drink, a couple of ice cubes and some hundred-proof Grand-Dad. Yet it seemed better when she did it.

She was one of his two prized tenants who made the hotel their permanent residents. Both had apartments on the sixth floor, hers just two doors down, and Roberta's at the other end of the hall. Roberta had come along with the hotel, and Toni a couple of years later. He charged them a hundred bucks each week for their apartments. And he knew that they each had a trick that they would only have to see once a week to get rent money.

"I had Beth call me when you started up," she said as he tasted his drink, the Grand-Dad burning his throat at first then leaving a sort of soothing sensation.

She had a key to his place, as he did to hers, and

32

she was welcome to use anything in his pad she wished. They never interfered when the other had visitors, nor did either make any demands. It was a beautiful relationship, he had often thought. It certainly was not love. If it was love, he could not stand to let her stay in the business. If it was love, he would not be hopping in bed with other women. If it was love, they would be married by now with a house full of crumb crushers. No, not love, simply a damn good working friendship.

"I tried to get in to see you, but you know Doc Matt."

"Yeah, Wes told me the same thing." He walked across the red shag rug to the bar. He sat his glass down on the counter top, slipped off his coat and threw it across to the black leather couch that matched the tops of the four bar stools.

She was right beside him, her breasts brushing against his arm. "Have a rough night?"

"Naw, Doc Matt's famous sleeping compound saw to that."

He half sat on one of the stools, getting his drink, as she took the first swallow of hers. It would be Scotch and soda he knew, on a fifty-fifty basis.

"What really happened? I talked to Ed last night, but I wasn't able to catch up with Vern."

He ran it down to her, not leaving out the bit about the bearded dude, but because the cops had not released the info, asking her not to spread it around. "I just left Hamilton, and we both got our tail feathers a little ruffled."

"I'd like to see you and Hamilton get together when that didn't happen."

He finished his drink, sat his glass back down. "Well, that's all history now. Let the cops play their silly games. I'm out of it."

"You mean it?" she asked. Was there a pleading look in her big brown eyes, asking him to stay clear of the trouble that would certainly be there? Maybe he was reading too much in her expression, seeing what he wanted to see, something to tell him that he was right not to get further involved.

For a moment, there was a picture of another pair of brown eyes, of a woman he had met only last night and who had died before he could help her.

He took Toni's drink from her, embracing her waist and pulling her closer to him. To hell with Alicia and the cops.

The kiss was long, warm, tender. He still sat upon the stool, and her hips were firm against the inner parts of his thighs. He was aware of the fresh bath scent of her, of the fragrance of lilac which was her favorite bath oil. He let his hands slip down over her ass, to the hem of her dress, to the warm flesh of her thighs. Back up under the dress then—and it was as he thought, she was wearing nothing else. He felt himself come alive with the moment, as he worked the dress up about her waist. Pulling her closer, it was as though he could feel the imprint of her matted hair through his clothing. She shivered, her arms around his neck. He kissed the tip of her nose, her eyes, her neck, the lobe of her right ear, she once told him it had given her all kinds of hell when she pierced it.

Pierced. That was it. Remembering was like

winning a hundred dollar pot with a pair of deuces, gratifying and yet surprising. But he had remembered. The dude last night in the bar had had a pierced ear.

He relaxed his hold on her, slowly began pushing her away. Her big brown eyes blinked at him. "What's the matter?"

"Cool it for a minute, huh baby? I just thought of something important. I've got to make a phone call."

"Phone call? You crazy?"

"Naw, really, it's important. I've got to get in touch with Vern."

She stepped back adjusting her dress, nodding. "Okay, Mr. Jerome Benson, you make your phone call." Her tone was cool, clipped. Whenever she got mad, she seemed to want to demonstrate how well she could control it. Calling him Jerome was the tip-off. His mother and sister were the only two people who regularly referred to him by his given name. When Toni used it, she was angry.

He reached out. "It'll only take a minute."

She knocked his hand away. "Sorry, I haven't got the time to spare," she said, turning and walking out of the apartment.

He could wait and call Vern later. He should go after her now and patch things up. But calling was important.

He went over to the couch, to the phone that sat on a stand next to it, dialed.

The phone only rang once before it was answered. "Hello-o," Marge greeted him, practically singing the word.

"Hi, doll, where's that no good husband of yours?"

"Bull! He's sleeping right now, got in kind of late. You okay?"

"Sure, some people are just too ornery for anything serious to happen to them. How's the twins?"

"As bad as ever. Ron had a fight in school yesterday, and Don had a fight with the same boy this morning."

He laughed. "Sounds like the same kind of stuff their old man and I used to pull. I hate to do it, but could you get Vern to the phone? I remembered something about last night I hadn't told him."

"Sure thing, Bull, just a minute."

There was drowsiness in Vern's voice when he first came to the phone, but it quickly went away.

"Pierced, huh? You sure?"

"Yeah, yeah. The right ear. I was pretty fouled up last night and forgot all about it. Think it'll help?"

"I'm sure it will, Bull, although it doesn't mean anything to me right now. Maybe one of the other boys have stumbled across something. Look, let me call the precinct and see if they got anything, I'll buzz you right back."

He replaced the receiver, went back to the bar. He fixed himself another drink, got a cigar from the silver humidor that sat on the corner of the bar. A pierced ear. There were the different cultures in the neighborhood, African, Arab, Indian, for all of whom the wearing of jewelry was not looked down on. It could be the sign of a big time player or pimp. A dude would fall out in a two C note suit, a half a C on his feet, and be sporting a diamond earring in one ear. But most commonly, a pierced ear was the sign of the younger gang set. It was a sort of badge of manhood, an open challenge for anyone foolish enough to make a joke about it. There was a gang on the West side, he knew, that used the pierced ear and a single ruby earring for just that purpose.

He was on his third drink, and nearly finished with his cigar when Vern called.

"Mason and Dorant's been working on it this morning," Vern said. "They came up with her address after a check from her credit cards. Joint on the West side, 3317 Kormanton. She had a room-mate, a Sharon Woods. They didn't get much out of her, felt she was dummying up on them. She said Alicia has a brother, Larry, but she didn't know how to get in touch with him."

"They didn't get very much."

"They're still working on it. Alicia had a gig as a sales girl at a novelty store downtown. They've got to check that out, see if they can get a lead on any of the people she hung around with."

"I thought things would be moving faster."

"Sometimes it does," Vern answered.

"What about the pierced ear? Did you come up with anything on that."

"Only guess work, Bull. I batted it around with the boys at the precinct. Have you heard of Tom-Tom Green?"

He thought for a moment, but could not recall the name. "I'm drawing blanks, Vern."

"What about the Black Renegades?"

It was the gang he had thought of earlier. "Off-shoot of the African Lords street gang."

"Yeah, that's them. Mean bunch of bastards but we haven't been able to pin anything substantial on them yet.

"Who's Tom-Tom Green?"

"One of their captains. He was due to appear in court today to start trial for working a guy over. He didn't show."

He did not ask Vern how all this tied back to Alicia. He knew Vern would just be guessing on most of it. The dude with the beard was not wearing an earring at the lounge, and a pierced ear did not mean he was a member of the Renegades. Yet the Renegades had been the gang he had thought about, the ones who wore the red ruby earrings. For Vern to hit upon the same gang could be a coincidence, but a gambler learns not to believe in coincidences.

CHAPTER

5

He did not try to catch up with Toni, but showered and dressed thinking about his conversation with Vern. Alicia, Tom-Tom Green, the Renegades. What was the connection, if any? Did Alicia have anything to do with Green's disappearance? And why would Green jump bail on a battery beef anyway? He probably would have gotten only a few months at the most, if he was convicted.

There was too much that he could not answer. He needed more info on the game before he started to play, and when he came in, he was coming in right. It was what he really wanted to do. He realized he was just fooling himself by saying he was going to stay clear of it. He wanted the bastard that killed Alicia. Good girl, bad girl, whatever the hell she had been, she did not deserve to be blown away like that.

There were maybe a dozen people in the lounge when he came into the joint. Some of the tables were taken up and four dudes were scattered along the bar. Isaac Hayes's "Shaft" was playing softly on the juke box, if the heavy rock beat could be described as soft at any volume.

Sam Devlin, the regular bar keep, was behind the bar, wiping the counter top, the ever present wooden match stuck in the corner of his mouth.

"Glad to see you've stopped faking, and back to work," Bull said, going up to the bar.

"I can't be gone for a day without you gettin' inta trouble," Sam said in his raspy voice. He had pushed the hell out of sixty. He was skinny, short, bald, his dark skin so tight about his head it seemed to make his eyes bulge.

"I didn't want you to stay off sick forever, figured this was the quickest way to get you back."

"Yeah sure," Sam said, smiling.

"How's the cold?"

"Down to a sniffle," Sam answered. "And that brain container of yours?"

"It's okay," he said. He had known Sam for nearly twenty years. It was Sam who had schooled him on the wonders of a deck of cards. Sam had been damn good at one time, he could make a deck of cards sing. But old age cooled all that, he lost the touch. He was lucky to get one note now, let alone the whole deck singing.

Sam had been the first person he hired when he took over the hotel. He did not consider it charity, just trying to pay back some of what was owed.

"Wanna shot?" Sam asked. "On the house. I knows the cat that owns this dump, he won't mind."

He laughed. "Later. I've got some running to do. If anybody important comes looking for me, tell'em I'll be back by six."

He left it up to Sam to judge who was important and who was not.

He kept his Caddy at the small parking area in back of the lounge. It was a year-old El Dorado, gold with black vinyl top. It was the third Caddy he had owned, and the first one he was able to pay cash for.

The ride to the West side and Floyd Hines's shop took twenty minutes traveling the Tri-City expressway. The shop sat in a part of the city that was a carbon of his own neighborhood. The buildings were old, dirty brick monsters. Most should have been torn down years ago. They should have been torn down back when he was a kid. Instead they were subdivided, cramming in more families, making some landlord's bank account fatter.

The shop was a basement deal, with the stairs running parallel to its picture window. The words ODDS & ENDS were barely readable upon the window, not so much due to the dirty glass but to the fact that the lettering was old and the paint had peeled. All sorts of objects jammed the window. There was a tricycle without handlebars, a flowered hat box, a pile or two of clothing, flashlights, a fishing pole, there was even an old copy of *Playboy* resting upside down in the middle of the whole mess.

The mustiness of the place filled his nostrils as he entered, and he puffed harder on his cigar in an effort to nullify the odor. It was like a trip to the junk yard. There was no counter, no set arrangement of merchandise on display, just junk piled here and there. A pair of ancient refrigerators with spiral-ribbed motors on top sat against the wall to his right. Half a dozen tires lay in the middle of the floor as though they had been stacked, knocked over, and no one had bothered to straighten them. A few old lamps, boxes, a metal cabinet, more clothing, and a wooden bucket cluttered the rest of the place.

"Hey, Bull," Floyd said, coming through the curtained archway at the back wall. "What's ta ya, man?" There was a butt of a cigarette in the corner of his mouth, a beer can in one hand. He extended the other as he stepped over a stack of newspapers coming towards him.

Floyd's hand was somewhat smaller than his own. He was a nickel and dime fence, dealing mainly with the teen gangs and small time punks that the street bred. A V of hair grew under his lower lip. His T-shirt and jeans were as wrinkled and dirty as everything else in the place.

He really did not like Floyd. He did not like the way Floyd made his living, helping kids learn how to steal, encouraging them, always slick enough to cover himself. He felt Floyd was doing more harm to the black youth of the city than any white bigot ever could. But he tolerated Floyd only because at times he was useful.

"Come on, cop a squat," Floyd said, digging a wooden chair out from behind some boxes. "Can I get ya a beer or something?"

"That's all right," he said, not wanting to trust his clothing to the antique of a chair Floyd had uncovered. The last time he had sat in this place, he ripped a thirty dollar pair of slacks, plus a hunk of his ass.

Back then he had been checking on a typewriter and a couple of adding machines that were lifted from his office. Floyd had said he knew nothing of the theft, but had been able to come up with the stolen articles in less than three hours.

Floyd shrugged, took a swig of his beer. "I saw the papers this morning. That anything to do with your visit?"

He nodded. "Yeah, kind of. What do you know about the Black Renegades?"

"The Renegades, huh?" Floyd said, his mouth pushed out somewhat. "Tough little bunch, Bull, plenty tough."

"That I know myself. What I want is the inside stuff, their structure, their aims."

"Well, hell, I know'em all, Bull. Known'em for years." He fiddled with his goatee. "Was it the Renegades last night?"

"I don't know. They might not have anything to do with it at all."

"Maybe not, but I wouldn't go making any wild bets against it."

Floyd was being cagey. He seemed never to be able to come up with an answer without going through a series of evasive jabber.

It was another thing he did not like about him.

"What'd you mean?"

Floyd took another swallow of beer, wiping his mouth with the back of his hand. "That chick that got offed last night. Her brother Larry's one of 'em."

He puffed harder on his cigar, putting a cloud of smoke between himself and Floyd. Again, it did not mean that the dude last night was a member of the Renegades, but the deal was beginning to stack up that way. "Run the rest of it down to me, Floyd."

"Sure," Floyd said, belching. "Well, ah, most of what I tell ya, is just what I hear 'round. The Renegades and me don't do that much business anymore. They've moved away from the kind of small time operation I'm running. Ya know me, Bull, I'm lucky ta be able ta keep a few coins in my pockets," he said, looking about his place in an apparent attempt to add truth to his statement.

"Yeah, sure, Floyd," he said. There were thousands of two-bit hoods who never made it, that hustled just to stay alive. But he placed Floyd along with the junk man who used to travel the neighborhood when he was a kid. The raggediest junk man with the most beat up wagon had the biggest house and the longest car. He figured Floyd had been stashing his dough away for years.

"Word is that one of the big boys have taken an interest in the Renegades," Floyd continued.

"Any names?"

He shrugged. "Sammy Major is what I hear, don't know for sure."

Sammy Major. He knew the name, the rep that went with it. Major, a black dude, was an ex-trigger man who had worked his way to one of the lower command positions in the city's crime network. It was said that Major owned the Greater South Side Towel and Linen Company, which serviced his hotel. The company was servicing the hotel when he took over, but he had never had any dealings with Major directly.

"Well, true or not, they stop bringing in stuff for me ta handle." Floyd drained his beer, stuffed his cigarette butt into the empty can. "I asked 'round a bit, got what I told ya, and backed off. Hell, I don't need ta get messed up with Major and his crowd, they only know one way to play."

Things were becoming more involved. If he was to believe Floyd, and there was no reason to disbelieve the bulk of what he was saying, a solution might not be that damn simple. The Renegades were bad enough. With Major as their teacher they could cop the training and finesse that separates the punks from the big leaguers.

"What about Tom-Tom Green?"

"Hey, now there's a good name," Floyd said with a smile. "I didn't know you were on ta him." He leaned forward somewhat. "You sure ya don't have all this written down somewhere and you using me ta verify it?"

45

"Sure I have," he said, not digging Floyd's drift, but when you come to play poker you play poker. "So do me a favor and verify."

Floyd shrugged. "Sure. Well, depending on how ya count, Tom-Tom is number two or three with the Renegades. There's maybe five or six hundred of 'em scattered 'round, with four dudes in control. There's Dex Patten, Bo Roberts, Tank Garmine, and Tom-Tom. They were the main ones who broke with the African Lords when the Lords got religion." He laughed. "That was a little over a year ago. Damn, they sure put a dent in my business then. I was doing good until the Lords decided to go with this black thing, helping their brothers and sisters make somethin' of themselves. What a stupid play, ya know. I mean what chance have we niggers got in this world unless we take what we want?"

He simply nodded, not wanting to get into any debates. He had strong divisions on the subject within himself. He knew the hopelessness of the streets, the filth, the poor education, the odds against the kids coming up. He knew why they were angry, why they felt they had to demand, to take. Well, taking was not the answer, no more than sitting back and getting screwed. There had to be a point in between, just where he did not know. If he had the answer, maybe he and Hamilton would not piss each other off as they always did.

"Anyway, the split came," Floyd said, "with a few heads getting busted. Lee Jones of the Lords wound up in the hospital. He's still running them though, gets mentioned in the papers a lot.

"Dex kept dealing with me, and as the Renegades got bigger, I began eating decent again. Larry was one of the new ones that came along. He hadn't belonged ta the Lords. Alicia was part of the package. She became Renegade property. She was a nice piece," Floyd said, smiling as he nodded. "You know how it is? The boys and me were tight, so they let me sample. A mellow lay, man, really mellow. Then Tom-Tom took her for his, and that was the end of my freebies."

There was an urge to flatten Floyd and tap dance on his chest. Merely not liking him had not produced this feeling before. Hearing him talk about Alicia that way was the trigger. But he held back, took long deep breaths. Floyd was being helpful. He did not want to ice that now.

"Okay, Floyd, then here's the big one. Why would the Renegades want Alicia dead, and would her brother sit still for it?"

Again Floyd scratched at his goatee. "Well, man, now we really don't know the Renegades did it, do we? I mean, that cat last night could've been after you."

"Naw, I went that round with the cops. If he wanted me, he had time to make sure. But he did put three slugs into Alicia."

Floyd nodded. "Yeah, well okay. Alicia he wanted, Alicia he got. But who knows, Bull? The way some of these punks are nowadays, they'd bust a cap on ya for a dime."

He had to agree. There was hardly a week that passed that the newspapers did not report a knifing or shooting that was teen-gang related. New York had the problem back in the fifties. The same problem was here now.

He had discussed it many times with Vern. They had done their share when they were teens, and the gangs then did not take any shit. But a killing then was rare, now it was practically the norm, in a recruitment drive or simply to re-establish one's might.

New York had solved her problem by containing it. They virtually let the gangs kill each other off until the surviving members reached adulthood, breaking with their gang loyalty. Some had stayed with the crime bit, some had not, but the big teen gangs were finished.

The main difference now was that back in New York most of the gang members were white and here they were black. With the civil rights things, the mixture of hate and frustration, the cries of get the pig, a whole new game had been set up. And there was a hell of a lot of commotion from all sides as to how to combat it.

"It could have been a rival gang," Floyd continued. "You know, out for revenge or somethin'."

"The African Lords?"

Floyd shrugged. "Naw, I don't think so. I doubt if their love for their black brothers extends to the Renegades, but killing ain't their scene. Don't know who it might be, though, I'll have to do some digging around, if ya want?"

He was wondering when it would come, Floyd

usually worked it into the conversation somehow. If the Renegades had a rival gang, ten to one Floyd knew them as well as he knew the Renegades. He took his money clip out, counted a hundred and thirty-seven dollars, and handed fifty over to Floyd. "Check it out. If you need any more let me know. But I've got a feeling the Renegades are responsible."

"Maybe, Bull," Floyd said, sticking the money in his back pocket. "If they are, Larry didn't know anything about it. There was just the two of 'em, you know. She was oldest, took care of him when their folks died. Don't think he liked it at first when she became Renegade property. Never said anything about it as far as I know, just a notion I got."

"Any idea where I can run him down?" he asked, remembering that Alicia's roommate had not been able to give that information to the police.

Floyd shook his head. "Only at their headquarters, that's the only place I've been able to catch up with any of them."

Again he felt Floyd was holding back. There must have been some other place he had met with the Renegades besides here or their headquarters. Floyd had gotten a little taste of his money and was probably laying plans to get more. It was to be expected, and if he got the answers he wanted he did not mind paying for them.

CHAPTER

6

It was late afternoon.

The headquarters of the Renegades was a little over three blocks from Floyd's shop, on Hastings just off Maurl Boulevard. The middle strip of Maurl, which was supposed to be green and growing, was more of a dirt pile than anything else. There were trees and a few patches of grass around to break the pattern of barren land but they did no good. It had been the same when he was a kid, on the South side around Caditon Boulevard. Too many years of baseball, football, and a hundred other games kids play had gotten the grounds into

50

its poor condition. Lack of interest by the city was keeping it that way.

He parked across the street from the headquarters, which was a converted store, its show window painted over. BLACK RENEGADES stood out in foot-high lettering on a red background. Their emblem, a black fist holding a spear, was just below the name. A battered, dark green VW sat at the curb in front of the place. Some light-skinned dude with a high Afro leaning against the front fender gave him a long look, then turned away.

He did not rush into the place, but sat in his Caddy, letting things line up in his mind. Alicia was Tom-Tom Green's girl. Now Alicia was dead, and Tom-Tom was missing. Tom-Tom was a leader of the Renegades. Alicia's brother, Larry, was a member of the Renegades. The dude in the bar last night had a pierced ear. All the Renegades have pierced ears. It kept coming back to the Renegades.

He was not sure just what he expected to accomplish by coming here. Certainly, none of the Renegades were going to race to admit killing Alicia, asking him to please turn them in. But they somehow were deeply involved. If they did not do it, then it was because of them it was done. What few facts he had gathered hinted at this conclusion his gambler's instinct told him he was right. And damn it, there was still Sammy Major to consider.

The scent of garlic was the first thing he noticed when he got out of the car. He saw the hot dog vendor, complete with chef hat, on the corner of the next block. Steam was coming from the open hatch of his push cart as he served the two boys before him. The street was beginning to fill. People were coming home from work, hitting the bars, going to the stores. The kids were out playing, the girls with their jump ropes and dolls, the boys with their penny pitching and a football that was so lumpy it must have been stuffed with newspaper.

He made it across the street with a stud in a Chevy blowing his horn at him as he sped by. Maybe the stud was mad that he had not hit him

"Move pretty good for a big man," the dude against the VW said. He was a Renegade, the ruby earring he was wearing told him that. There was an edge in his voice.

"I weighed nine pounds when I was born, man, and I came out running." He tried never to let anyone get up on him about anything.

"You got business over here, or somethin'?"

Mentally, he dressed him in a black jacket and dark pants. He put the stubby beard on him, messed his hair. The guy was slightly built, a slackness in his clean-shaven face. His eyes were a mite too big, too rounded. The high Afro standing even about his head seemed freshly done. He could have been the one last night, but he was not sure.

"Yeah, I've got business here. Where's Larry Hill?" He figured that if he was going to get any help at all from the Renegades, Alicia's brother would be the one to catch up with.

The dude shrugged. "He ain't here, big man. Ain't seen him for a week."

"I'll check for myself."

The dude shrugged again. "Hell, go ahead. Dex is inside, ask 'em for the fifty-cent tour. 'Course, for an important man like Bull Benson, he might not charge you anything."

With his picture all over the front page of today's *Challenger*, being recognized was not a surprise. He just wondered if reading the *Challenger* was a daily routine for the Renegades, or was today's issue of special interest to them. Then thinking about it more, he could not place too much importance on it either way. With Alicia being so involved with the Renegades, he doubted if there was a gang member who had not read the *Challenger*.

"You got my label, what's yours?"

"Marv Fellows, big man," he answered.

"I'll remember that."

"Hell," Marv said, with a crooked smile upon his thin lips. "Before I'm finished with this world, a lot of people going to remember."

Another punk's cry for recognition. He had heard it expressed a thousand different times by a thousand different guys, but maybe never quite as sincerely. Marv Fellows, whether he was the dude last night or not, was definitely someone to watch out for.

He was confronted with huge posters of Angela, Malcolm, King, and Brown as he came into the place. They covered the walls in varied poses, from serene stares to angry shouts. The clinched fist and spear emblem of the Renegades occupied the middle of the back wall. Three dudes sat at a small table before it. They were looking at him.

The one on his left was high yellow, with a nappy Afro and a thin trace of a mustache under his pointed nose. The one in the middle was of chocolate brown complexion, with thick bushy eyebrows that almost made his narrow eyes seem non-existent. The one on his right was somewhere in-between the other two as far as complexion was concerned, but he easily outweighed both of them combined. His flat nose, protruding lower lipped face was a rounded mass of flesh. His Afro was so high, it almost looked like a wig. And he had a pair of shoulders that seemed equal to the gorilla's housed at the city zoo. All three wore one ruby earring.

It did not take much balls coming into the place. He was not expecting trouble, maybe a little hot language. He would lay ten to five that the Renegades had everything from zips to baby howitzers stashed in the joints. But it was even a better bet to figure that with the cops hawking the Renegades, the weapons were damn well hid and not all that easy to get to. So if it came right down to it, it would be with fists, and he was an old alley fighter from way back. Yet he was aware that Marv had come in, closing the door behind him, and he moved over some to his left to keep them all in his view.

There was an issue of the *Challenger* lying on the table before the three. The guy in the middle tapped ashes onto the floor from the butt of a cigarette, stuck it back into his mouth. "What'd ya want, Benson?"

"He says he looking for Larry, Dex," Marv answered from his position against the door. "Tol'em he ain't here."

So the one in the middle was Dex Patten, head of the Renegades. Three to two the big stud on the right was Tank Garmine. His size demanded a name like that. And it was even money that the other dude was Bo Roberts. Here were the leaders of the Renegades, with the exception of Tom-Tom Green. He wondered if they always stuck together, or had the shooting called for a special meeting.

"You heard the man, Benson. Bo and Tank here will back that up," Dex said. "We ain't seen Larry in a week."

At least he was right about the names. "Nobody seen Larry for a week, huh?" he said. "Well, you've got that part of your story together."

"What's that suppose to mean, Benson?" Dex asked, the butt of the cigarette almost down to nothing.

"I think the man's saying we's lying," Tank said, his lower lip sticking out farther, and he began to crack the knuckles of his chunky hands.

"I ain't saying nobody's lying," he said. An argument now would not help. He had to get a lead on Larry Hill. "Look. I almost got blown away last night. Alicia Hill did. Maybe ya don't give a damn about it, but I do."

"We give a damn, Benson," Dex said, finally putting the cigarette out in an ash tray on the table. "Alicia was one of ours, and we'll settle it ourselves."

Now where was he coming from, a gang rival bit, or an internal struggle? Dex was not the dude last night. He was too dark, and Tank was too big. He imagined the scrappy beard on Bo, but again he was not sure, and wondered if he would ever be able to recognize the dude again. "Anytime my ass is on the line like that, then I've got to know who, and why."

Bo scratched at his pointed nose. "If Dex says ya stay out, man, ya stays out."

"Shit if I will. I want the son of a bitching bastard that killed Alicia. I want to know where Larry is, and I want some answers now. Like what has Sammy Major got to do with all of this?"

Bo stopped playing with his nose. Tank stopped cracking his knuckles. They all looked at him intently.

Dex nodded. "For a stud that's supposed to be pretty hip, you come on like a pig. Tank, show the man out."

It was like releasing a trained watch dog. Tank sprang from the table at him on the run, arms swinging. He side-stepped the first punch, which caught him high on his left shoulder knocking him back onto the wall.

If Tank had any advantage it was not in size, maybe in youth and speed. But experience has a way of making up for a lot of that.

Tank came in on him, jabbing lefts at his head. One punch landed on his bandaged wound, setting off a shock wave of pain. Tank must have seen that it hurt, because he started smiling. His lower lip widened in the smile until it did not protrude, and he kept directing more punches at the bandage.

He blocked most of the stuff Tank threw at him, waiting for the opening to show.

"Handle the son of a bitch," Dex said.

"Do him a job," echoed Marv.

He could see them gathering about, getting closer. They were allowing Tank enough room to work, but they probably wanted a piece of him before Tank finished the job.

Last night he had not been able to do a damn thing about the dude in the phone booth. Today he had held back when talking to Hamilton and Floyd, because it would have been a stupid play. But the Renegades had not given him a choice, and he was glad. He was glad at the chance to hit back.

He blocked a looping hook with his left and chopped down at Tank's lower lip. He felt flesh and teeth merge under his fist, as the blow snapped Tank's head to one side.

"Watch that bastard," Dex said. "Don't let him hit you again."

He caught Tank with a left to his stomach and a right to his chin that staggered him backwards. Tank was not smiling anymore, his eyes watery, blood coming from both corners of his mouth. Carelessness lost as many fights as lack of knowledge. He was not going to give the Renegades anything to gloat about. He took his time coming in on Tank, picking his shots. A left to the jaw, a faked right, a jab just below the heart were the type of combinations he threw.

He opened a cut over Tank's left eye. A left by Tank brushed against his right cheek. He slammed an overhand right to Tank's flattened nose. Blood shot from both nostrils. Tank blinked, cursed, and swung wildly. He ducked, rammed a left into Tank's stomach, then came up hard and fast with a right uppercut that sent Tank across the room onto the wall.

Bo jumped him then with a tackle, but the dude was just too light to make it work. He broke the hold quickly, not wanting the others to get it into their heads that a joint effort would be better. He lifted Bo by his shirt collar, and folded him with the hardest right he could muster.

Tank was coming back now, slower than before, more open. He blocked Tank's wide right, hooked his arm around it and held him there, shooting three quick ones to the face. Marv made a move, and he flung Tank's limp body into him. The two landed in a tangled pile on the floor.

It left only Dex and him standing, Dex's narrow-eyed glare so intense, it seemed that he was trying to wish him dead.

There was a stinging sensation coming from his bandaged wound. He was aware of his own heartbeat, the quick, harsh breaths he was taking. Yet he felt better now than he had felt all day.

"Ya know your life ain't worth a thimble full of shit now, Benson. Ya didn't just come in here and mess with the brothers a little bit. Man, ya messed with the Renegades."

"I only wanted to talk, Dex, you set the rules."

Marv was standing now. "Let me fix'em, Dex."

"Don't be silly, Marv. You can't handle me bare

handed, and I'll cream'ya before you can dig anything out of its hiding place."

"Ice it for now, Marv," Dex said. "There's plenty
of time. We'll get even."

Bo had gotten to his feet, holding his jaw. Tank
was moving about on the floor, coming out of it.

"Marv, Bo, give Tank a hand," Dex said. "Benson, you get your ass out of here."

"I still haven't got my answers."

"You've got all you're going ta get," Dex said.

"Looks like he's been giving more than he got,"
Tommy Mason said from the doorway.

Mason came into the place with Vic Dorant following him. They were a salt-and-pepper team that
worked out of the Moore Street Precinct. He did
not consider them close friends or enemies. They
had a rep on the street as being tough but fair.
Vern had said they were working on the shooting.
Being here meant they had tied Alicia to the Renegades.

"What's been happening, Bull?" Dorant asked.
"Local trials for the golden gloves?" He was a
squat built guy, his blond hair mixed with gray.

"Naw, that big clown over there just tripped over
his own feet."

"Sure he did," Mason said grinning, contrasting
clean white teeth with a somewhat ashy black face.
"Which one's Patten?"

"That's me, pig. What'd ya want?"

"Just a talk for now, punk. How'd you want it?
Here, or at the station?"

"I ain't going ta nobody's station."

59

Mason shrugged his beefy shoulders. "Fine with me, as long as you feel like talking."

"I don't think we'll be needing you, Bull," Dorant said, motioning him with a nod towards the door.

"Okay," he said. "Dex, I'll be getting back to you."

"That's definite, Benson."

Dorant stopped him as he was going out, leaned forward. "You know we've got to tell the lieutenant about you being here."

"Play the cards that come to you, Vic."

Dorant nodded. "Just so you know."

"Thanks."

Now Hamilton would have something else to bitch about. Well, let the white bastard get in a sweat over it. Maybe he would have a heart attack. He could not let himself worry about that now. He was thinking too much of the reaction he got when he mentioned Sammy Major.

Floyd had been right about that one. They would not have gotten so uptight, if they were not mixed in with Major. He would have to go slow now. Be very careful, or Alicia would have him for company in the morgue.

CHAPTER

7

The kids were still outside with their dolls and lumpy football, but the hot dog vendor had gone. He walked between the battered VW and the rust-colored Ford that everyone on his side of town knew was the car Mason and Dorant used.

He was about to enter his Caddy when he heard someone call him. He swung around to see Forest Westerfield approaching.

"Glad to see you dealt yourself into this thing, Bull. I'm going to have some story for the *Challenger* when it all straightens out," he said, pushing his glasses back onto his nose.

"The dude who shot Alicia dealt me in."

Wes nodded, his broad mouth stern. "I was at the precinct when Mason and Dorant left to come out here. I didn't expect to see you walk out of that damn place. Did you get anything worthwhile?"

"A little exercise," he said, rubbing the knuckles of his right fist.

Another nod from Wes. "Who's in there?"

"The big boys, Dex, Bo, Tank, some dude named Marv Fellows."

"No sign of this Larry Hill, huh?" Wes asked.

"None. How did you find out about him?"

"Mason tipped me at the precinct. That's why I followed them out. How does it read to you so far?"

"Hell, I'm not even ready to start guessing." He pulled a cigar out of his breast pocket, offered Wes one that was refused.

"Don't think I'm being pushy, Bull. It's just that this old news hound in me doesn't allow me to hold a civil conversation without it sounding like the third degree. Hell, if I wasn't hanging around here for Mason and Dorant I'd buy you a drink."

"No harm, Wes. As for the drink, I'm heading back for my place now. Meet me later and we'll crack a bottle."

"Sounds beautiful. Catch you later, then."

He watched Wes walk back towards his own car, then hopped into his Caddy, kicked the engine on. He had tied Alicia to the Renegades with the information he got from Floyd. He wondered how

Mason and Dorant learned about the connection. What had led Vern to ask him about the Renegades in the first place?

The early evening crowd was there when he got back to the lounge, half filling the place. Aretha's "Day Dreaming" was floating from the juke box, setting the mood. It was an oldie but it fitted, soft and light, the type of music for this time of day— the after-work-unwinding period.

He made his way to the bar greeting people at the booths and tables along the way. Gus and Hank from the body shop down the street were there, Mable from the beauty parlor on the corner, a young intern and a nurse from Jayburn Community waved at him from a back booth.

He stood by one of the empty stools at the bar as Sam waited on a customer down at the other end.

"Oh, hello, Bull," Sid McFadden said, from the stool next to him. He was a dumpy little guy, balding, his features too large for his dark face.

"Hello, Mr. McFadden, how's it going?"

"Okay, Bull. Say, I heard about last night."

"Yeah, everybody has."

McFadden was a salesman in a men's clothing store over on Broome Street. He always conducted himself in a way that the Mister tag seemed natural. Scotch and soda was his drink, and he was in the place about three times a week. A quiet dude who never bothered anyone, a nice dude it seemed, and that was the way he had had him pegged. But McFadden was a fooler. It was not until last December that his impression of McFadden had changed. He had placed some football bets with Davey, the queer, at Mr. Fanny's Cafe. McFadden had been sitting in a back booth, complete with false eyelashes, lipstick, and a pink jump suit. He did not believe McFadden had seen him, and he had never mentioned it to anyone. What the hell, it was McFadden's life, he could do what he wanted with it.

"Well, it's good to see you weren't hurt too badly, Bull," McFadden said, looking up at him then quickly turning to his drink on the counter. "I can't imagine the Bull Pen Lounge without you around to run it."

He laughed. "I can't either."

McFadden turned back to him, his big muddled brown eyes seemed fixed upon his face. "I mean, that is—"

Sam came up sliding a drink across the bar to him. "Ya looks thirsty," he said.

McFadden turned back to his drink again.

Some hard rock was coming out of the juke box now, a tune he could not recall hearing before. He tasted the Grand-Dad cooled by the ice cubes, holding the liquor in his mouth before swallowing.

"Anybody drop by today?"

"Vern n' some white cat's in the office now," Sam said, with a nod of his bald head. "Been waitin' most of a hour. Business type. Kind of slick, if'n ya ask me."

"No name?" It was not like Vern to set up surprises.

"Vern didn't bother ta introduce us."

He finished his drink, let the liquor play inside him for awhile. "Guess I'd better go check'em out then. Take it easy, Mr. McFadden."

Vern was sitting on his desk when he came into the office, playing cards with the white dude that occupied the chair at the corner. They both had helped themselves to his humidor, nubs of cigars sticking in their mouths.

"Come back in a half hour, Bull," Vern said, looking at his cards. "I'm already working on his next year's salary."

"No, don't," the white dude said, throwing the cards down onto the desk. "I'm glad someone arrived to stop this slaughter. The way he's been winning, I'm beginning to think those damn cards are marked."

Vern yelled his laughter. "Hell, man, they are. I thought you'd catch on sooner than this."

"Damn you, Vern," the white guy said, smiling. He was somewhere in his twenties. His thick matted black hair contrasted sharply with his complexion. His clean-shaven face was lean, hard. The suit he wore was a brown double-breasted pinstripe, with matching vest. Sam was right, he had the look of a business man, but what kind of business? And why had Vern brought him here?

Vern stood. "Bull, I'd like for you to meet Harlan Ralinski from the D.A.'s office. He was handling the case against Tom-Tom Green."

Ralinski stood and they shook hands, a firmer grip than he had expected. A handshake is supposed to be a greeting. But most of the time with him, maybe it was because of his size, people always seemed to be trying to prove something. He had given up playing those games years ago.

He walked around his desk, sat in his padded leather swivel chair. "Can I offer you fellas anything else? More cigars, a drink, something to eat?"

"No thanks, Bull," Vern said.

"Just put these cards back wherever Vern found them," Ralinski said, pushing the deck towards him.

"I only keep 'em around for a joke," he said, gathering the cards together. "Don't want anyone from the D.A.'s office thinking I actually use these things."

"Whatever you do with them is your concern, Mr. Benson, as long as I never see them again," Ralinski said, and he glanced over at Vern, who was still smiling at him.

He put the cards away, took two last puffs on his cigar before putting it out, as Vern and Ralinski resumed their original sitting positions.

"You know all those guys?" Ralinski asked, indicating the framed pictures that hung on every wall of the dark oak paneled office.

There were pictures of him shaking hands with various sports figures. Some were taken in the lounge, others at different sports events. The bulk consisted of boxers and football greats or near greats. "I know most of 'em well enough to get a few bucks if needed," he said. "But I doubt if Vern got you here to clean you with my cards or to show you my pictures. So if you don't mind, Mr.

Ralinski, I would like to know what this is about."

"You're a rather direct man, Mr. Benson," Ralinski said, then looked over to Vern.

"I guess I'll start," Vern said, taking the cigar out of his mouth. "Hal has already spoken with the lieutenant. He's made a connection between Green and Alicia—"

"I know the connection," he said, "and about her brother too."

"How the hell did you know that?" Ralinski asked, around the nub of a cigar.

"I told you he wouldn't be sitting still on this."

"I was by the Renegades' place," he said, for an explanation. It was not the time to bring Floyd's name into this. Maybe later, when he and Vern could talk it over alone. "I ran into Mason and Dorant on my way out. Hamilton probably knows I was there by now."

"Well, you know what kind of reaction that's going to get," Vern said, rubbing his jaw, his lips slightly out-pushed.

"I've thought about it."

"Okay, the lieutenant just about had Hal convinced you've got more to do with this thing than you've said."

"And now you believe I'm innocent, Mr. Ralinski? Why?"

Ralinski sat up straighter in his chair, put his cigar out in the tray with the others. His eyes seemed to narrow, his lean jaws appeared to harden more. "I haven't made any decisions, Mr. Benson. Vern asked me to come here and talk with you. I owe him a favor, so here I am.

Also this intrigues me. He and Lieutenant Hamilton are as rigid in their opposite opinions of you as any two viewpoints can be. It's quite curious."

"It's not all that curious, Mr. Ralinski. Basically it comes down to being black and white."

"Are you saying that Vern's only taking your side because you're both black?"

"Naw, it's the other way around. Hamilton is on my ass because I'm black."

"That's difficult to digest, Mr. Benson. From what I know of Lieutenant Hamilton's record, he's spent the majority of his time on the force working in the black communities."

"What better place for a bigoted bastard," he said.

Ralinski's gaze went from him to Vern, back to him again, a slight nod of the head. "What about it, Vern?"

Vern scratched at the corner of his thin mustache. "The lieutenant's a damn good cop," Vern said, then paused. "I don't know if I'd swallow the bigot idea, but there's no question about his feelings towards Bull. He wants Bull behind bars. Not for any little shitty beef, but for something that will get him some good time."

Another nod from Ralinski, frowning, several lines stretched across his forehead. "And you, Mr. Benson? What's your feelings about Lieutenant Hamilton, for whites in general?"

"I wouldn't let Hamilton clean my toilet," he said, then added mainly because Ralinski was beginning to tick him off, "I guess maybe there are

68

one or two whites around who are not trying to screw everybody else in the world."

Ralinski was smiling, a cocky little thing that curled up the right corner of his mouth. "Tell me, Mr. Benson, who's the bigot now?"

"From my chair, it's still Hamilton," he said, ignoring Ralinski's point. Hamilton must have done a thorough job in that talk he and Ralinski had earlier.

Ralinski stood. His smile was gone. "It's been interesting, Mr. Benson. You coming, Vern? This conversation's gone as far as I think it can."

"Slow down, Hal," Vern said, holding a hand up. "Didn't we get a little sidetracked? I told you they didn't like each other from the start. Maybe I didn't stress it enough. Alicia Hill is dead, and Tom-Tom Green is missing. We came here to exchange some ideas, and maybe get a few leads, remember?"

Ralinski sighed, a deep slow sigh. "All right." He sat back down. "A couple of months ago, Mr. Benson, Tom-Tom Green was arrested on a battery charge. He almost killed a bartender one night who refused to serve him. Green's twenty-two but looks younger. Besides he was slightly intoxicated when he came into the place.

"He gave the arresting officers a lot of trouble too, so when they got him to the precinct they threw him in one of the solitary confinement cells. You know how those things are, a little eight by eight bare box, no window, no light."

He had heard about them, he knew dudes who

had spent some time in the piss holes. It was the hardest time they spent in jail, alone, nothing to do, no room to do it in.

"Most of the guys at the precinct knew Green was a member of the Renegades. A call was put in to the D.A.'s office and that's how I came into it. Well, I was surprised as hell when I got there. Green was claustrophobic, he was cracking up in that solitary cell. I saw a chance that a lot of people in this city have been looking for, a chance to break up the Renegades."

There seemed to be a glow about Ralinski's face, a brightness in his eyes. He was back at the precinct, recounting the scene and evidently enjoying it.

"I promised Green I'd get him five years in a solitary cell if he didn't come across with information on the Renegades," Ralinski continued. "I didn't think he would go for it, but I guess the fear of that cell was the realest thing to him. I've got a seventy-five page affidavit of names, dates, crimes they were involved in, plans.

"We worked it this way. I got Green his lawyer, a court-appointed public defender. I told Green to tell the others that the public defender would be best instead of getting their own lawyer, because the case would be easy enough to win. Then every time Green went to see the public defender, I was there to get more information for the affidavit. It was really working beautifully."

"It sounds like you had the dude's balls in a vice," he said, more than mildly irritated. He wondered how many similar scenes took place in the precinct houses throughout the city. How many dudes had been screwed into jail terms out of fear.

"Do you know how many people the Renegades have by the balls?" Ralinski asked, leaning forward in his chair.

"Yeah, but aren't ya suppose to do things by the letter of the law and all that."

"Fuck the letter of the law where trash like the Renegades are concerned!"

He laughed lightly. Ralinski was not the only one who knew how to bait someone. "Now who's the bigot, Mr. Ralinski?"

Ralinski's lean face reddened.

"Don't play with me, Benson." he said, pointing a finger. "Lieutenant Hamilton can't give you one tenth the trouble I can."

"I'm about to wet my pants," he replied sharply, and as coldly as possible, looking at Ralinski directly.

"Hold it, you two," Vern said. "I'm no goddamn referee. I didn't come here for that. I think it's time we had that drink, Bull."

He got a fifth of Grand-Dad and three glasses from a bottom desk drawer. It was the old fire for fire bit. Ralinski had come on him hard, but he had gotten down harder. He had made use of the practice himself more than once. He would be in a card game and discover someone was cheating, and would have to start cheating also as a manner of self-defense.

Ralinski tasted his drink, took a deeper swallow, then sat the glass down. He looked around the office. "You really know all these guys, huh?"

"Yeah," he said, waiting for Ralinski to start their verbal boxing match again.

Ralinski nodded. "I'm beginning to understand Lieutenant Hamilton a little better now. You're not an easy man to like, Mr. Benson."

"I'm not an easy man to push around, Mr. Ralinski."

Ralinski raised his glass, smiling slightly. "Well," he said.

"In Green's affidavit, did he mention the name Sammy Major?"

"How the hell did you turn that one up?" Vern asked.

"Just something that came to me today."

Ralinski nodded slowly. "Yes, he mentioned Major. But Major was too smart to deal with the Renegades personally. He used one of his boys, Windy Wright, as the go-between. All the business was done through this Wright character. That's one of the reasons we wanted to take our time on this thing, hoping maybe something else might break. The plans were for us to drop all charges against Green at the trial yesterday. Then, with court immunity, remand him over to the crime commission for public hearings. It was felt that some indictments might come out of the hearings. But if nothing else, we were sure that the hearings would disrupt the Renegades and Major's operation enough to finish both of them in this city."

"Well, you've still got the affidavit," he said. "Why not start the hearings anyway?"

"It's not quite that simple, Mr. Benson. The affidavit isn't signed. As afraid of that jail cell as he was, Green absolutely refused to sign. He figured that once he signed, if he was killed, the affidavit would still hold up in court. Without him around to verify the affidavit it was just a bunch of paper. So not signing was like a life insurance policy, to make sure we gave him protection."

"And did you?"

"We tried, up until last Friday afternoon when he left his lawyer's office and gave my men the slip."

"So now Green's girl is dead, and he's missing, and that leaves you kind of up shit's creek, doesn't it, Mr. Ralinski?"

Another long slow nod. "That's right, Mr. Benson," Ralinski said. "I've read your police statement. Was that the way it happened, nothing left out?"

"That was everything, with the exception of the pierced ear that I phoned and told Vern about."

"You got any ideas on all this?"

He sweetened his drink, added a splash or two to the others. "Well, I've never seen Green, but it's a safe bet that the dude in the lounge last night wasn't him. Alicia had a good view of the door, and she was probably casing everybody that came into the joint. She would have recognized Green regardless of how he looked. So, if the dude last night was a Renegade, he was one she did not know that well, or not at all.

"We know she was hiding. The question is why? No one tried to snatch her and make her talk, so she was killed so she wouldn't talk. Now would Green kill his girl so she wouldn't tell where he was hiding? That doesn't sound right to me. No, my money's on Green already being dead. She knew it, and that's why she was killed."

"Yeah," said Vern, as he raised his glass. "That's the way we figured it, too."

CHAPTER

He had dinner, worked the bar for about an hour, and went back to his office to go over last week's invoices. All the while he thought of Alicia, of her death and his summation, and of Vern's agreeing with him. Tom-Tom Green was dead, and Alicia was hit because she knew it. Even Hamilton believed that according to Vern. Except that Hamilton had *him* pegged as the cause of it all, or as the finger man at the very least.

The only way he was going to get Hamilton off his back was to find out who did kill Alicia, and that he had already vowed to do.

The knock was so faint at the door that he almost did not hear it. "Yes, come in."

She was a skinny doll, tall and bony. Her hair, which was evidently a wig, was jet black, long and lustrous about her face. She wore a lot of eye make-up accenting her rather small eyes. There was a hint of blush on her cheeks which blended in with her dark complexion, and her thin lips were slightly pinked. Usually women wearing too much make-up turned him off. He would rather see a broad with none on at all than one who botched up the job. Yet the woman in his office did not look that bad. Her make-up had been applied with care, even though a little heavy-handed. Her outfit, a blue midi and jacket with white boots and a large white purse slung over her shoulder, seemed to take away from her boniness.

"Mr. Benson?"

"That's me, baby." Whores were always popping in, trying to get him to be their sponsor. Damn, Hamilton would love it if he turned the hotel into a full-fledged cat house. The joint would have a pad-lock on it within a half hour.

"I'm Sharon Woods," she said. "Alicia's room-mate."

Her arrival was not totally a surprise. True, he had not thought about her coming here, or about her at all, frankly. But he knew a lot of people simply did not like talking to cops. He had acted as go-between before. His friendship with Vern and a few other dudes on the force was widespread knowledge.

"Have a seat, Miss Woods," he said, motioning to the chair before his desk. And once she had sat, "Now what can I do for you?"

She licked her lips, leaving them moist and shining, as she looked about the room, back at the door that had swung closed by itself, back to him. Her expression seemed drawn, rigid, as though she was forcing herself not to show any emotions. "I bet there's half a dozen cops outside watching this place."

"Could be," he answered. "And maybe some of the people who handled Alicia too." He had not concerned himself with that too much. But once saying it, he realized it could be true.

She sat her purse on her lap, opened it. "Damn," she said practically to herself, closing the purse as quickly as she opened it. "Do you have a cigarette? I chain-smoked mine on the way over here."

"Sorry, doll, I'm a cigar man, myself," he said, pointing to the cigar butts that rested in the ash tray on his desk. "I can get you a pack from up front, if you want? What's the brand?"

"No," she shook her head. "Thanks. I'm smoking too much anyway." She clasped her hands over her purse, took a deep breath. "Really, the whole thing right now is I'm just nervous."

"A drink, then," he offered. "Nothing helps nerves better than a jolt of strong booze."

She shook her head again. "No. I'll just say what I came here to say, and get the hell out."

"However you want it," he said. People who came to him like this wanted to talk on their own

77

terms, set their own rules. Sometimes he did not have the patience for it, now he could not afford not to.

"I didn't tell the cops none of this," she started, licking her lips again.

"I know what you told the cops," he said.

She looked at him directly for a moment, then nodded. "Yes, I guess you would. And you probably know about Alicia, and Tom-Tom, and the Renegades."

"Some of the highlights."

She smiled, nothing big, but the first sign of movement on the otherwise stone face. "I'm beginning to wonder why I came here."

"Me too, doll, what's the answer?" He said it lightly, not forcing.

She shrugged, straightened the purse on her lap. "Alicia was my friend. I'd like to see whoever done this to her caught. I'd like to help, if I can." She paused. "Without getting myself in trouble."

He felt it was an honest answer. She wanted to help, but only if she could do it without getting involved, only if it could be done without putting her neck on the line. People rarely told such truths about themselves. She gained a couple of points from him for that.

"Maybe it'll be easier if I ask you the questions?"

"Yeah, it probably would," she said.

"Okay, fine. When did you see Alicia last?"

"Friday morning, when we were getting ready for work."

"No talk about what she had planned for that day, no contact with her since?"

"No, none."

"Did it bother you that she didn't return over the weekend?"

"No, of course not. You know how it is," she said with another shrug. "Sometimes I didn't come home for the weekends."

"Yeah, I can dig it," he answered. "When was the last time you saw Tom-Tom?"

"Oh, last Wednesday. He was over for dinner."

"Just the three of you?"

"Well," she started, glanced down at her hands, back to him. "No, Dex was with him."

"You and Dex got a thing?" he asked, for the first time beginning to doubt her. Dex could have sent her here with some nice little story just to keep things confused.

"Let's say Dex and me ain't strangers, huh."

"Okay," he said. He would not push it, but he would not forget it either. "Did you talk about Tom-Tom's upcoming trial?"

"Not much, Tom-Tom didn't want to. He said the public defender was pretty mellow, and that he didn't have a thing to worry about."

"What about Alicia's brother, when was the last time you saw him?"

"Larry? Oh, a week, a week and a half, something like that. I never knew when he would show."

"You told the cops you didn't know where Larry was staying. How true was that?"

"Well, it was pretty close to the truth, I don't know where he is. He floated a lot, even stayed at our place a few times. When Alicia wanted to see him, she usually got in touch through the Renegades."

He leaned back in his chair, rocking slightly. She really was not telling him anything useful, nothing that would start turning the odds in his favor. Maybe she did not know anymore. Maybe if she had the answers, she would have gotten wasted along with Alicia.

"Has Larry, or any of the other Renegades, tried to get in touch with you this weekend, or since Alicia's death?"

"Just Dex. He called this afternoon. Told me don't worry, lay cool, and he and the Renegades would even things for Alicia."

"Did he tell you who he suspected of making the hit?"

"No."

"Then can you tell me why you don't believe him? Why you've come to me?"

She looked at him directly again, her slender shoulders raised and lowered in a deep sigh. She licked her lips. "I don't know what kind of trouble Alicia was in, but I do know she came to you for help. She'd been wanting to meet you ever since they did that story on you about helping that dude out of that murder rap. She thought you were pretty heavy. *The* Big Bull Benson! You've got a rep that covers this city. Who knows, if Tom-Tom didn't have her on such a tight leash, you might have caught up with her a long time ago.

"Anyway, she had troubles bad enough to get her killed. If she knew things were that rough, she'd go to the Renegades first for help. If her trouble was with the Renegades, and she couldn't go to them, I figure she'd turn to you."

"Yeah," he said, "and what a beautiful job I did." He had seen the possibility right away, that Alicia had come to him for his help. Now he knew for sure that she had. And he had promptly paraded her out in front of her killer. If she had only told him when she first came into his bar, he could have stashed her so well no one could have gotten to her. If he had only reacted sooner to that dude in the phone booth, instead of thinking of her, and bed, and a night of fun and games.

"Was there anything else?" he asked.

"No, I guess not," she said.

He poured himself a double Grand-Dad after she left, finishing it in one hefty swallow. Having it confirmed that Alicia coming to his place last night was not an accident did not set too well with him.

He was pouring himself another drink when the phone rang. There was an extension at the bar out front, but most of the calls were generally for him. So he did most of the answering.

"Bull? It's me, Wes."

"Oh, hey, Wes, what happened to you?"

"That's why I called. Some dude chopped his old lady up, and I got trapped to cover the story. Can I get a rain-check on that drink?"

"Hell sure, anytime. Say, how did Mason and Dorant make out?"

"Zeroes, big fat ones. Those Renegades got a long history of not co-operating with the law."

He really had not expected anything else. "They share any ideas with you?"

Wes laughed. "Say, who's supposed to be pumping who? I'm the reporter remember?"

"Sure, Wes, I remember. I only want to find out what you know, so I won't be telling ya the same things over again. You know, so I can just fill in the gaps."

"Bull, that's the biggest load of crap I've heard since the mayor announced his inner city redevelopment program."

He had to laugh himself this time. "Truth is, Wes, I'm not ready to talk yet. I've still got some things to piece together. When I'm set, you've already got my word that you'll be the one I talk to."

"Hell, Bull, if I doubted your word, I might as well stop putting my teeth under my pillow waiting for the tooth fairy to bring me a quarter."

"You bastard," he laughed.

"Yeah, ain't I. Anyway, Mason and Dorant weren't speculating too much when they left the Renegades. They're going to be tearing the city apart trying to find Tom-Tom Green and Larry Hill though. A young hotshot from the D.A.'s office tipped them to the connection, dude named Ralinski. Know him?"

"We've met," he said.

"That's about all I've got, Bull."

"Thanks, Wes." He could have added "for nothing," because when he put together what Wes and

Sharon Woods had told him, that was what he had, nothing.

He went back to checking invoices. Besides the murder, the Renegades, Hamilton, there was still the business of running a hotel and lounge to be taken care of. The phone rang again. Damnit.

"Yeah?"

"Hey, man, who pulled your tail?" It was Floyd, that super-hip voice of his was not to be mistaken even on the phone.

"Yeah, Floyd, what have ya got?" Maybe he had actually learned something.

"Hey, baby, I've really been busy. Told ya I ain't been in touch with the Renegades for awhile. Well, I learned some things that even surprised me. Hell, man, I ain't been surprised in over a year since when I found that cherry. Didn't think there was anymore left in the world. She's working out on Maynard Street now, maybe ya know her—"

"Ice it, will ya, Floyd. I heard enough about your love life last time."

"Yeah, okay, sure, Bull. Let's see, Tom-Tom Green is missing. He never showed on a two-bit court case yesterday morning. But I guess ya know that."

"I'm not paying you to find out what I know."

He detected a slight laughter along with Floyd's answer of, "Yeah, yeah, ya're right, man. I got most of my info from Tank. Me and him had a couple of beers after you and the cops paid him and the boys your visit. They ain't sure if'n ya had the cops waiting outside ta back ya up all along, or if things just fell that way. Anyhow, they going ta be on ya case now, baby. They don't like the way ya came in on them. I'd watch myself, Bull. I think Tank and Dex are both a little nuts.

"Tank says, they don't know where Tom-Tom split to. They haven't seen him since Sunday night, when they all got together to decide if they should go to court with him. Tom-Tom talked them out of coming along and they haven't seen the dude since."

Floyd had certainly gotten more from the Renegades than he had. But the story Tank had whipped on Floyd varied just enough so that it would not jive smoothly with the theory he and Vern had come up with. They had figured Alicia had gone into hiding because she knew Tom-Tom Green was dead, but Green had been seen Sunday, and Alicia had checked into the Lairmont Friday night.

"What do you know about Marv Fellows?" he asked. There was something gnawing at him about the dude.

"He's new with the Renegades. That's just about it, Bull, why?"

"Nothing much. What's the word on Larry Hill?"

"Tank saw him yesterday afternoon, loaned him a few bucks. Said he was trying ta catch up with his sister but hadn't been able ta."

Yesterday afternoon Alicia was still at the Lairmont Hotel, waiting for nightfall, waiting to come and ask him for help. "Did Larry have any idea where Alicia was?"

"Tank didn't say so."

"Does he know where Larry is?"

"Naw, none of 'em do. Larry trips out a lot. He's probably holed up somewheres with a giant high working."

"What d'ya mean? You didn't tell me Larry was on the shit."

"I forgot it, man, really. He was always cool with it, always had enough dough to keep hisself mellow."

"Okay, Floyd, but I gave you good money for good information, I don't want nothing half-assed about it."

"Damn, Bull, fifty bucks don't buy me."

"And fifty bucks won't take care of your hospital bill if you start fucking me around." Some people had to get hit in the head with a brick before they stopped being cute and quit playing games.

"Okay, okay, so I made a mistake, man. But ya did promise me more dough."

"Only if the info is straight, Floyd, remember that. What's the Renegades' thinking on Alicia?"

"One of two things. Either the Lords are trying a power play ta take over the neighborhood. Or Tom-Tom is the one that busted a cap on her, and they're not sure why."

"All right, you got anything else?"

"Naw, that's it, man."

"Okay, call me when you do."

He had not known how annoyed he had gotten with Floyd until he hung up. Then he realized how heavy he was breathing, and recognized the urge within him to swing at something, or someone. He could recall quite easily what Floyd had said about Alicia earlier, and the manner in which he said it. It was not a tranquil thought, but he could not brew about in his own little world of hate.

He took a cigar from the humidor on his desk. The tobacco was strong and good. He had a thick white cloud floating lazily before him on his second puff. Emotions had to be locked up. Sound, clear thinking was what he had to do. He had to look carefully at what Floyd told him, see if there was one or two points that would hook it all together with the way he and Vern had figured the deal had gone down.

The phone rang. He felt like tearing the damn wires out of the wall. The times that he would welcome the interruptions they never come. He started to ignore it, but hell, if it was answered up front and it was for him, Sam would buzz him over the intercom anyway.

"Let me speak to Bull Benson." It was a man, talking low, almost a whisper.

"You got him, brother, what's up?"

"You sure you're Benson?"

"What the hell ya want, my jock strap size or something? I'm Benson. Who are you?"

"Hill," the voice came through the phone, still at a whisper. "Larry Hill, I've got to see you."

It was five minutes to ten when he parked at the address on Riter Avenue that Larry Hill had given him. This stretch of Riter still showed its battle scars from the riots a few years back. There seemed to be just as many vacant lots as there were buildings. The buildings that were still standing were just barely doing it. Most, like the one he was parked in front of, had its first floor boarded up with condemned signs posted on the worn wooden slats, and even in those that were occupied, there were only a few lighted windows. The local alderman, a black dude named Pyne, had been petitioning the city for the past several months to do something about the fire-traps. As always, where poor folks were concerned, the city was moving with its usual swiftness, and had not done a damn thing.

A light, warm breeze brushed over him as he got out of his Caddy, kicking up a spark from the tip of his cigar and carrying a swirling stream of smoke away from him. He was quite conscious of the weight of the snub-nosed .38 in the waistband of his trousers. He did not like carrying a gun. For one, there was no such thing as a permit to carry a gun in this city unless you were a policeman or guard or something like that. Hamilton would love catching up with him right now. Then there was something that Sam had told him many years ago. "If'n ya carries a gun, ya're apt ta use it. A gambler an' a gun ain't a smart team. Either he runs inta somebody else wit' a gun, or the cops. The odds just ain't worth coming up against." Yet there were times that he did carry the gun. Times like now, when he was to meet in a condemned building with someone who might or might not be Larry Hill, for reasons that might or might not be the ones that were stated. "I know who killed my sister," Hill had said. "I want you ta help me fix the bastard. But we can't talk over the phone." Then he had been given the address, with instructions to come alone.

He had thought about telling Vern, but knew it would not work. Whoever was in the building waiting for him, whether it was Larry or some dude planning to waste him, all they had to do was see that he was not alone, or suspect it, and they would split. He would never learn who was in the building that way, and if it was Larry, he might lose his chance for good to contact him. Of course he had thought of one other possibility, that it was Larry and Larry was waiting to kill him.

He puffed hard on his cigar. The street was quiet. There were only four or five cars parked on the entire block, none whose looks came close to the appearance of his Caddy. An old truck sat crookedly on milk crates or bricks in the middle of the vacant lot across the street, the door on the driver's side open and hanging on one hinge.

The wall artists had gotten to the building, their gang names and mottoes were scribbled all over. The Gangster Lovers, the Almighty Ethiopian War Gods, the Black Bats. A lot of people had gotten their two-bits in. The words over-lapped, blotted each other out, and were squeezed between each other. A sprinkle of old-fashioned curses balanced the whole thing.

He had been told to use the side basement entrance. There was enough light for him to see that someone had written on the door in runny red lettering, "pussy power." "Right on," he said, sliding the gun out of his waist band, then turned the door knob and stepped in.

He could not see a thing, but the smell reminded him of Floyd's shop, it was that same musty closeness. He dropped his cigar to the floor, crushed it out, took a pencil flashlight from his jacket pocket. The light from the little flash darted about the room at his direction. The wall artists had been here too, they had even gotten to the floor and ceiling. Trash and cardboard boxes were scattered about, and a battered stained mattress lay in one corner.

The meet was to be on the third floor, room 304, and the instructions were for him to use the back staircase because it was closer. He found the back staircase, the pencil flash guiding him over more dust and rubble through the narrow hallway. The building seemed quieter than the street, tomb-like. It was a hell of a choice of words, yet they were the right ones. He could not even detect any rats running about in the walls.

He noticed that his hands were sweating, and he tightened his grip on the gun as he started up the stairs, listening, looking into the darkness beyond the flash. First floor. Second floor. Nothing. No one had greeted him, no one had taken a shot at him, no one had tried to drop a bomb on his head. And as quiet as he tried to be, the only sound he heard was his own footsteps on the old staircase. Third floor, jackpot, bingo.

He trained the light down the hall which was lined with doors and covered with dust. A straight-back chair lay on its side half in, half out of one of the rooms a few doors down. He turned the light to the door nearest him on his left, 305. Room 304 was across the hall.

He stood to the side of the door, knocked, listened, knocked again. "Larry. Larry Hill, it's me, Bull Benson."

Silence was his only answer. He tried the door knob, still standing to one side, not exposing himself. The knob turned freely, and he pushed the door inward, listening, waiting, but nothing happened. What the hell was this turning into? He looked into the room, the pencil flash revealing its only occupant, a white metal table sitting just off the center of the floor. He stood in the doorway, looking the room over again. It was as if he was trying to prove that the room was not empty, that Larry was in a corner, or would come popping out of the wall someplace.

The door behind him squeaked, and he dove into the room, managing to turn the flash off before he hit the floor with his hands and knees. Maybe his reaction was due to his memory of what had happened the last time a door opened behind his back. Or maybe it was just hearing a sound in the building that he did not make that scared the shit out of him. Whatever, he did not care. The main thing was that he got out of the way as three slugs came charging in and buried themselves into the wall across from the doorway.

He lay on the floor, his gun and pencil flash extended before him. He thought he was pointed towards the doorway, but he could not be sure, and he could not risk turning the flash on just yet. It was quiet again, the burnt scent of the cordite faintly drifting about him. He began to wish he had not come alone.

Footsteps, two long strides from the direction he was pointed. He tightened up on the trigger and the button of his flash. The room exploded with gunfire. Three more slugs came in after him, one striking the floor just to his right. He turned the flash on, squeezing off a couple of shots on his own, the .38 jumping in his hand. He snapped the flash off, rolling to his left until he hit the wall.

More footsteps now, running. The staircase.

He was up, the flash back on, the gun ready. He got to the staircase in time for the small beam of the flash to catch someone in a dark jacket and slacks darting out of sight on the basement floor.

He sat across the desk from Lieutenant Hamilton in his office at the Moore Street Precinct. Crawling around on that floor had not done his clothes any good. He had tried brushing himself off but the dirt seemed to have woven itself into the fabric.

There was a frown on Hamilton's thick-lipped face, his bald head reflecting the glow from the neon fixtures in the ceiling. Vern and Charlie were there too. Vern sat in a chair at the side of the desk, while Charlie stood just behind Hamilton on his left, partially blocking a picture of the police commissioner hanging on the wall. He had been in Hamilton's office quite often. The place never seemed to change, there were the same dull gray walls, the same dark green filing cabinets, the same faded maps of the city and of the Moore Street Precinct boundaries. There was even, usually, the same group gathered. He and Vern against Hamilton and Charlie was the way it usually ran, sometimes just him alone.

"You come up with more crap than any one person I've known, Benson," Hamilton said, pointing a finger at him. "But let me tell you something.

Subterfuge hasn't worked with me before, and it won't now."

"Well, you pick up on this, Hamilton. I said I was shot at. That's two days in a row that someone's bust a cap in my direction, and tonight that dude was definitely after me." He did not really think he could come to the precinct without having a run-in with Hamilton. He had hoped only that he could get here, tell Vern what had happened, and split before Hamilton saw him. But it had not worked out that way. Charlie was in Hamilton's office a moment after he stepped into the squad room. Maybe it would have been better if he had simply phoned Vern.

He did not have the time to be bothered with Hamilton right now. Someone had tried to kill him tonight. It might or might not have been the person that got Alicia. Back at that condemned building when he had turned the flash on, he really had not seen anyone, firing blindly, and the guy on the stairs was gone before he could even get a good idea of his build. But getting shot at meant someone believed he knew too much, or was getting too close to proving some of the things he suspected.

"Last night you just didn't duck fast enough," Hamilton said. "And tonight's just another episode in our Bull Benson fairy tale."

"Hold it, Lieutenant," Charlie said, with a nod of his square-chinned face. "Maybe Bull here ain't lying. Why don't ya lay it all on us, Bull. Ya set-up the broad last night, now your pals ain't so sure 'bout ya, and decided ta put a zipper on that trap of yours. Now he's running ta us for protection. Well, we don't hand out that kind of service, not unless ya want to sign a confession and give us the names of those in this thing with ya."

"You're not really that damn stupid, are you, Charlie? Or are ya just trying to let Hamilton know how tough ya can sound?"

Charlie glared down at him from across the desk, his jowls puffed out more than normal. "Listen, punk, I'll break your goddamn neck trying ta get smart with me."

"Save it for the nickel and dimers out on the street, Charlie, maybe you can impress them." Threats did not mean a thing with the positions they occupied. But if Charlie came from around that desk, he was going to dump him on Hamilton's lap.

"Can't we save all of this for right now, Lieutenant?" Vern asked. "You know it'll be easy enough to find out if Bull is telling the truth."

Hamilton nodded, a big smile broadening his thick lips. Charlie still stood behind him, puffing hard, his fists balled at his sides. "That's right, Sergeant. Don't let things get too rough for your buddy, here."

Vern glanced at him, then back to Hamilton. "How many times have I got to make myself clear on the matter, Lieutenant?"

"How many times have I got to make myself clear, Sergeant?" Hamilton's smile was gone, and he had began tapping a finger onto his desk. "Benson here is no better than the scum we pull in here every day, he's just been luckier. Sure, we'll put a call in to the Roosevelt Street Precinct and have them check the building, but what will it prove, maybe that somebody's been shooting holes in the wall? Who's to say that Benson didn't do that himself? You hadn't thought about it that way, have you, Sergeant? No of course not. Well I have, and Charlie has, and any good policeman should."

Hamilton had a way of grinding in a point when he had the upper hand.

"I have my own views, and I make my own decisions," Vern said.

"Okay, then," Hamilton said. "Assuming Benson is telling the truth. Just how do you think he got out of the trap?" Hamilton turned away from Vern. "All you told us, Benson, is that you were lured to the third floor, shot at, and that your assailant got away before you got a good look at him, except that he was dressed similar to last night's gunman. So, what made him run away?"

He knew what Hamilton was fishing for, it was obvious as hell. "I just mentioned your name, Lieutenant, and the bastard went screaming down the stairs."

From the top of his starched white shirt collar to the top of his shiny bald head, Hamilton turned red. "Charlie, frisk that smart ass son of a bitch."

"With pleasure," Charlie mumbled, and came from around the desk. "Get up, Bull."

They would have to really be out of their skulls if they thought he would walk into a police station carrying a gun. He had stopped off at his lounge and given Sam the .38 before coming out here. But Hamilton and Charlie, he knew, were angry enough to hope that he still had the damn thing on him. Hoping they would have a good excuse to put him behind bars. And from Vern's expression, the slackness of his long face, his eyebrows hanging low over his eyes, maybe he was wishing that he never met a dude named Bull Benson.

"I said up," Charlie mumbled again.

He looked up at Charlie. Beads of perspiration had formed along Charlie's hairline, he had worked himself up. He could tell that Charlie really wanted him to resist the frisking. He still felt he could dump Charlie onto Hamilton's lap, but there was no need.

"Help yourself," he said standing, his hands raised.

Charlie did a rough and thorough job frisking him.

"He's clean, Lieutenant," Charlie said, with a hint of disappointment in his voice.

"Get his keys and search his car," Hamilton said. "And on your way out, have one of the boys put in a call to the Roosevelt Street Precinct."

He gave Charlie his car keys, and sat back down. "You mean you just might believe me, Lieutenant?"

"I mean we'll check it out, period."

Charlie closed the door behind him, and Vern said, "It was a stupid play you made going to that building by yourself, Bull."

"I know that now, Vern, better than—"

"Cut it, you two," Hamilton said. "I haven't bought the story yet. But I do know you were at the Renegades headquarters this afternoon, Benson. And I've already spoken to your buddy about bringing Ralinski over to see you behind my back. He's got the word, Benson. Any more cute tricks like that, and I'll have him doing the graveyard shift on the docks."

They went that route for another half hour, threatening, challenging each other. Charlie naturally did not find a gun in his Caddy, and the Roosevelt Street Precinct seemed to be taking their time in reporting back. He got his keys and went back to his hotel.

He went straight to Toni's room, by-passing the lounge and his own apartment. He did not feel like rapping with Sam or any of the customers in the lounge, nor did he feel like being alone. She answered the door dressed in a pale yellow negligee that was transparent enough to give glimpses of her body underneath.

"You busy?" he asked.

"Not until about one," she said, the little girl's face looking up at him. She had gotten rid of the pigtail, and her hair was long and fluffy about her head. Her full-lipped mouth was pushed in a pout, and her big brown eyes stared at him unblinkingly. "And what if I am free for now, Mr. Jerome Benson. Remember I'm still mad at you."

"Baby, get mad at me when you're on your rag, or when I've just been laid by the world's greatest nymph. But don't get mad when I've just come from bitching with Hamilton, or when somebody's been using me for target practice again."

She looked at him closely for the first time and at

his dirt-covered clothing, searching his face for maybe a hint of some sort of morbid joke. Then she nodded, "Come on in, I'll fix you a drink."

She had two bars, a long mahogany number in the living room, and a leather padded job in her bedroom. He followed her into the bedroom. The bar was only four feet wide, with enough counter space for a few bottles, some glasses, and a bucket of ice. It sat against the wall, next to the portable TV, under a poster showing the different love-making positions of the zodiac. The only light on in the room was a small lamp on the night stand by her oval queen-sized bed. The soft pink glow it gave off seemed to spotlight the bed, making it the focal point, and throwing the rest of the room into a shadowy dimness.

She mixed the drink, handed it to him. The sting of the Grand-Dad felt good. It was like a vital sign showing him he was still alive, that he had made it through another one. And it was not until then, when he began to relax, that he realized how tense he was.

"I should have known when you had to make that phone call to Vern this morning that you wouldn't stay out of it."

"I never really had a choice."

He walked over to the chest-of-drawers, took another swallow of his drink before sitting it down, and began taking off his clothes. By the time he had his things dumped onto the chair next to the chest-of-drawers Toni was in bed, her negligee hanging on the closet door.

He climbed in and she came to him, warm and

soft against him, smelling of lilac enhanced by her own body scent. She lay at his side with his arm about her, her head against his chest, as she gently pulled at the hairs on his stomach. This is where he should have been all along, not out playing cop, getting shot at, fighting with Hamilton. He kissed her forehead, squeezing her to him a little more, and he began telling her what had gone down since he last saw her.

She began rubbing his stomach, making slow wide circles as he told her about Floyd, the Renegades, the bad vibes he had gotten from Marv Fellows. She was rubbing his thighs now, back and forth, back and forth. He could have taken her then, he wanted to, but there was something nice about waiting, something nice about building the moment.

He condensed the story Ralinski had told him but lost track of what he was saying a couple of times. She had quit toying with his thighs and now had hold of him, gently massaging him with her finger tips. "Vern was saying—"

"Who's Vern?" she asked, kissing his neck.

"Who the hell cares," he said, swinging her around on top of him.

He was in her without any trouble, they were both ready. They lay still for a moment, he felt her heart beat against his bare chest. When they moved they moved together, stroke for stroke, in a rhythm they had had plenty of time to perfect. It was a slow, deliberate pace at first, building in tempo. She nibbled on his ear, kissed his eyes, his nose, his lips. She wore no lipstick but her lips

99

were still sweet, moist. Then he took charge, with his hands on her ass directing, controlling.

"Baby," she whispered in his ear. "Baby, god-damn."

When he relaxed she took over, handling it the way she wanted to in a whirling frenzy that brought him to the brink. Then they were back in union again, slow . . . fast, slow . . . fast, fast, fast, fast . . .

CHAPTER

10

He wore only his slacks and shirt when he left Toni, walking down the hall to his apartment barefooted, carrying his shoes and socks in one hand, his jacket slung over his shoulder. He could not begin to count the times he had left her apartment this way, or the times he had stayed. Being with her was never a routine deal, although they both were wised to each other's body, knew what was wanted, expected. It was a relationship with no strings. Yet a lot of times, he wondered about it. He really called the tune most of the time. But what could he say above that? She washed out the pressure and the troubles of a day like no one else could. She was a hell of a person, a hell of a woman, and he dug every bit of her.

He unlocked the door, stepped into his apartment, and was reaching for the light switch when something hit him on the back of his head. The blow knocked him to his knees, bright flashes of light danced around him. Someone's foot landed hard in his stomach. He doubled, falling forward, pain shooting in all directions. A fist smashed into his jaw, helping him to the floor. Someone jumped on top of him. He kicked, twisted, turned, swung out backhandedly. He felt his fist meeting someone's chin, forcing the head to snap back and a loud cry. He was hit and kicked again, but he had one of them by an arm. He was half on top of him, twisting the guy's arm behind his back. If nothing else he was going to get one of them, pull the damn thing out of its socket, if he could.

"Goddamnit, Dex, he's got my arm," a voice cried out. "Kill the mother-fucker before he breaks it."

Someone grabbed his head, twisting, pulling him back, nearly choking him. But he held on to the arm, applied more and more pressure. Someone tugged at his hands, trying to break the hold. He was cursed at, and then hit squarely in the mouth. He tasted blood, and the sting of a split lip. Another blow to the side of his head, and more until the stars were back and the whole damn world swung around before him.

Rows of gold sparkled through his shag rug as he came to. He was trying to figure who would beat him up and then leave gold dust for his hospital bill, until he realized it was just the pattern made by the sun coming through his Venetian blinds. He got up slowly because the room was not staying still for him. His head was pounding, and there was a deep emptiness in his stomach. He tripped over his shoe almost falling, but managed to make it to the bar. He half sat, half leaned against one of the stools while he poured himself a drink. He nearly spat the first swallow out, from the shock of the burn as the bourbon hit his split lip. He tested his teeth with his tongue. They were not loose or chipped, but his top lip was swollen. He downed the rest of his drink, feeling the bourbon as it traveled to his stomach. He stood, belched, the bourbon seemed to be boiling inside him. He got to the washroom just in time, and threw the whole thing up.

It took him an hour to get himself together. He showered, letting the warm spray beat upon his body to take away the soreness where he had been beaten. A couple cups of black coffee and some aspirins were for his head. He took inventory in the washroom mirror. Besides the swollen lip, he also had a swollen left jaw and a bloodshot left eye. Plus there was still the bandage he had gotten from Monday night. His mustache covered most of the swollen lip, and if he was smoking, his cigar would hide the rest. But there was not much he could do about the bloodshot eye or the swollen jaw, except make up a story.

It had definitely been the Renegades who worked him over last night, and that was puzzling.

Because that meant it had not been the Renegades who set him up at that condemned building. If it had, then they would have finished the job in his room. But they did not. So it was someone else in the building. But that did not make sense either. Who else was there?

Reporting it to Vern would not do any good right now. And paying another visit to the Renegades headquarters was out. If they were there, they were probably laying for him. But there were still two places for him to check out, the African Lords and Sammy Major. He felt he was coming close to the end, it was just a matter of straightening the pieces out.

The Lords occupied the third and top floor of the Blackland Community Recreation Center. He should not have been surprised at the contrast between their headquarters and that of the Renegades, yet he was. They were both on the West side, barely fifteen blocks separating them, but the similarities ended there.

He was greeted at the head of the stairs by a large oak desk, a dude in a bright green and red dashiki sitting at the desk, and a set of wooden double doors behind him. AFRICAN LORDS was engraved in a very flowery script on one door, and the names of its officers were on the other.

The guy at the desk looked up at him through rimless glasses. He was sporting a well groomed high Afro, and a fuzz of a goatee on his long narrow chin. The guy studied him with concern, it was easy to tell him from the frown on his face. But

104

then he relaxed a little, and came up with the black power salute and a smile. "Peace, brother, what's happening?"

He returned the salute, said, "I'd like to talk to Lee Jones, the name's Bull Benson."

"The man himself. You've been getting a lot of press time lately, brother."

"Yeah, I've got one of those faces that everybody goes for."

"Sure, brother, come with me. I think Lee's been expecting you anyway."

He followed the guy through the double doors into a brightly lit carpeted hallway. Doors and posters lined the hall. Some of the same people graced the walls here that were on the walls at the Renegades headquarters. Only here, Angela, Martin, and Malcolm were in quieter more peaceful poses. There were others too, like Crispus Attacks, Bunche, DuSable. And slogans of "people together," "unity is power" were on plaques between the posters.

The dude finally stopped in front of an unmarked door, knocked and opened it before anyone answered.

"Yeah, Steve, what's up?" He could not see who was talking because his view was blocked.

"I got a brother out here says he's Bull Benson, and he wants to see ya."

"Well, don't make him wait, Steve."

Steve stepped aside with a nod, and he walked in. The stud standing behind the desk in the narrow room was wearing a dashiki of the same basic color and design as Steve's. His Afro was also high and well groomed, but his glasses were gold rimmed, rose-colored grannys that sat at the end of his fat nose. "Mr. Benson," he said, extending his hand, "I'm Lee Jones."

They shook in the thumb-locked soul clasp that was supposed to mean unity. But he knew some who used it as just another way of getting to you.

"Please be seated, Mr. Benson." He sat on one of the wooden chairs before the desk, and Jones re-seated himself.

"You want me to leave?" Steve asked from the door.

"Sure, why not?"

"This dude's face don't look too cool. That's a recent job, brother, and he don't look too happy about it."

"Relax, I'm here to talk. You can stay or not, I don't care."

"I think I will hang around."

"Damn it, Steve, will you take your ass up front."

"Okay, Lee, okay, I'm just thinking 'bout you," Steve said, shrugging, and left the room.

Jones leaned back in his chair. "Damn, ever since we split from the Renegades Steve's been hovering over me like a mother hen."

The room was lined with old metal cabinets on one side and a couple of bare wooden benches on the other. All along the upper portion of the dull tan walls were posters announcing events the African Lords were sponsoring. They ran from community outings to live entertainment at the local lounges, and some were dated back to a year ago.

"I can understand his concern about the Renegades." He rubbed his jaw.

Jones straightened in his chair, seemed to be concentrating on his face. "Renegades do that?"

"It's a good bet." He paused. "Steve said you were expecting me."

"Well, not really, Mr. Benson. But the cops have been by, and I kind of guessed you'd be showing too. But I didn't expect you to've come from a fresh bout with the Renegades." Jones sighed. "Those dudes still play rough. I thought it would catch up with them by now."

"Maybe it has."

"Meaning you, Mr. Benson? You don't look much like a winner to me." Jones said with a slight smile.

"I hear you didn't look too great yourself after your set with the Renegades." There was no sense in going into any detail of his beating. He wanted Jones to open up. Maybe having something in common, like a beating from the Renegades, would do the trick.

Jones nodded. "Yeah, I was pretty fouled up. Those dudes really gave it to me. But you know, it was worth it. I mean look around, man. It's just been a little over a year, and the Lords are really moving. If a brother walks in off the street, I don't care what he's got, V.D. or a arm full of shit, we got somebody here that can help him. If you want to get your high school diploma, or maybe prepare yourself to enter med school, we can help. If a sister's been hooking all her life and she just don't know anything else to do, we can help her." Sweat

107

had began to sprout on Jones's forehead as he nearly preached about the Lords' accomplishments.

"Nobody's arguing about the good things the Lords have been doing," he said. "But there's a rumor going around that you're trying ta take over the streets again."

"Hey, no good," Jones said, yanking off his glasses. "Where'd you get that load of junk, man?"

"Indirectly from the Renegades."

"Well, does it make sense? After what I told you, does it? Man, we got the streets now, at least the unity and power of the decent element. I don't need to hassle the Renegades or any other gang, they gonna crumble. A unified community will see to that. We're taking young kids now and starting baseball and basketball teams before they get the notion to form a street gang. We're taking needles out of studs' arms and talking some sense into their heads. Show them somebody cares about their black asses."

He was getting a drift from Jones that he would not have put odds on when he first came up here. But underlining what Jones was saying was gang warfare. "Just what do you think the Renegades are going to do while the good elements of the community are squeezing them out?"

Jones sighed, licked his thin lips. "They won't like it, Mr. Benson. And frankly we expect some trouble, but we've had trouble before. I know what you're thinking, but we hung up the rough stuff when we split with the Renegades. There's other ways to get to the street gangs, man. We're going to bust every pusher in the black community. We're going to drop a dime to the cops on every crime we see or get wind of. The Renegades will get the message soon enough, they just can't win."

"Did you know that the Renegades have got syndicate backing now?"

Jones nodded. "I've heard it, but haven't heard any names mentioned. Hell, it's nothing new. The syndicate has always run the dope operation in the black community. They let some of us blacks front the deals, but they get the big dough."

He had to agree. It was an old story, but a true one. "Did you know Alicia Hill?"

"The chick that caught it Monday night? Naw, we never met. The cops asked me the same thing. I guess she must have got hooked up with Dex and the others after we split." Jones slipped his glasses back on, paused. "You know we really haven't broken away from the label that was slapped on us in the old days. We've done a hell of a lot of good things, Mr. Benson, but as soon as the Renegades make a little noise, the cops are back here checking us out."

"But it's not just a little noise this time."

Jones nodded. "Black folks killing black folks is nothing to take pride in. And believe me, the Lords are dedicated to stop it."

He came away from Lee Jones with a lot of admiration for the man. There was a young black trying to do something for his people. Just being around Jones made him check himself out, and he had to admit that his own contribution was lacking.

He also came away confused, because Jones

seemed to talk about the street gangs and the dope pushers as one and the same. The only connection he had known the Renegades had had with dope came from Floyd's remark that Larry Hill was hooked. And although Sammy Major worked for the syndicate, he had never heard of him dealing in dope.

Something was not fitting together.

Sammy Major had the penthouse apartment in the Roman Arms Tower, a twenty-seven floor steel and glass structure just off the lake. The joint featured a stone statue of a Roman soldier at the entrance of its drive, plus other statues and paintings of ancient Roman life throughout its halls. Music was piped into the self-operated elevator, the heavy horned type that is usually the background for the epic Roman movies. On the twenty-seventh floor, two hoods met him at the elevator, patted him down, then brought him in to see Major.

The room was spacious. One wall was mostly glass and it gave up a hell of a view of the lake, its greens and blues. He could see sailboats bobbing about so far away that they looked like toys. The carpet was white, thick and fluffy. The bar, which was on his right, was gold trimmed in black, with a gold-gilted mirror behind it. Two white couches faced each other over a gold coffee table. And there was a highly polished grand piano sitting on his left, just before a built-in false fireplace.

There was a guy sitting at the bar and one coming from behind it with his hand extended. "Well, Bull Benson. Funny we never got together before. I'm Sammy Major." He was thick-chested, wearing bell bottoms and a T-shirt. His sideburns and mustache was one continuing line of silver-gray hair that sprouted upwards into a full blown Afro. His smile was wide, toothy, possibly genuine. They shook hands, and Major took him by the arm steering him to the bar. "This here's Windy Wright, my ace," Major said, gesturing to the guy at the bar.

He and Wright exchanged nods. Wright was not what he really expected as being anybody's right-hand man. He looked like a cinch to take. He was tall, and lanky with a thin bony face and a pair of eyes that were small yet bulged. But Major would not have anyone around him that could not handle himself. So he decided that if any shit was thrown into the game, he was going for Wright first, hard and fast.

"Name your mouth wash, Bull," Major said, behind the bar once more.

"Grand-Dad, hundred."

Major nodded. "Good drink, think I'll try some of that maself."

Major fixed the two drinks, passed him his, Wright was still working on a half a glass of beer.

"Looks like ya lost an argument with somebody," Wright said.

"I've lost them before," he answered, focusing on Wright's eyes until the man blinked and turned back to his beer.

"I always appreciate social calls, but somethin' tells me this ain't sociable."

"It is and it isn't, Sammy."

"Fine," Major shrugged. "Now that clears up everything."

He smiled. Major was a likable dude. He wondered if Major, in his early days with the rackets, when he was a full-time hit man, joked with his victims before killing them.

"We both been in this city all our lives," Major said. "I've been hearin' 'bout you, guess you've been hearin' 'bout me. 'Cording to the papers some broad got shot out of your arms Monday night. Now here you show with your mug kind of disarranged, and I've got to ask maself if it all connects somehow. Or maybe I should ask you."

He took another swallow of the bourbon. "It connects in a way, Sammy," he said, forming in his mind the right way to put it. If his information about Major and the Renegades was correct, then he could expect anything from them, from lying to trying to kill him. If his information was wrong, well, Major's temper was known throughout the city, a smile one minute, ice the next. He knew himself that nothing pissed him off more than when he was telling the truth and someone would insist he was lying. He figured Major would be the same way. But whatever made Major mad, his reactions would be the same. He would have to play this scene very cool indeed.

"You've heard of the Black Renegades?" he asked.

Wright swung back around on his stool, sipping his beer. Major rubbed at his fat lower lip, nodded. "Bunch of West side punks ain't they?"

"Yeah, that's them. Well, I think they had something to do with that Monday night hit. And I know they did this job on me."

"So?" Major shrugged. "Why come see me?"

He paused for a moment. Both Major and Wright were intense in their stares upon him. It could all break loose right now, he thought, take it slow. "Well, Sammy, I've been getting some funny rumbles on the street. Word is you're taking the Renegades under your wing." And he decided to throw something else into the pot to test out Lee Jones's theory. "Word is you've got them pushing for ya."

"I'm what—" Major's laughter rocked within the room, he pounded the bar top, tears formed in his eyes. "Goddamn, Windy, did ya hear that? Me backing some street punks. Ain't that a blast?"

"Yeah, boss, I heard," Wright said, but his smile was a crooked little thing that was gone before it got started.

"Where'd you get this crap?" Major asked, wiping his eyes with the back of his hand, his body still heaving in laughter.

"Like I said, from the street. It didn't sound right ta me, so I thought I'd let you know."

"Thanks, Bull," Major said, still smiling as he took another drink. "God that's funny. Me, hooking up with a bunch of wet-nosed punks." Then he stopped, nodded slightly. "Slow down a minute. If you got the word, and those punks did that broad Monday night, then maybe the cops got the word too." He nodded again. "Now it stops being funny."

"I was thinking the same way, boss," Wright said, setting his beer down.

"I don't push no dope, Bull," Major said shrugging. "No moral bit. If a fool wants to kill himself with that crap let him go ahead. It's a business

113

where some good bucks can be made. I wished to hell I could get into it, but it's somebody else's territory. You don't cross lines in this outfit."

"Why waste time telling him that?" Wright said. "What we ought ta be doing is getting Benson here ta tell us who's been throwing that kind of talk around. Ain't right for somebody ta be using your name." And he ended it by slipping his hand inside his jacket, his mouth a downward curving line, his little eyes seemingly bulging more. It was a classic threatening gesture, and Wright handled it with the expertise of a master.

"That's a good idea, Windy," Major said. "Where'd you get your info, Bull?"

The wrong thing said or done just now, he knew, and he could quite easily be dead. "It was just a rumble, Sammy."

"The boss wants ta know where," Wright said, straightening his position on the stool somewhat.

"What good will it do if ya go and clobber some poor slob? Sammy, the dudes that talks to me don't talk ta the cops, anyway."

Major pushed his mouth out slightly. "Yeah," he nodded. "Yeah. You can relax, Windy. I'll go for that for now, Bull, but damnit, I better not get any heat from the cops." He pointed at him. "Got that, Bull? One word from the cops, and Windy'll be around to see you."

Wright was smiling now, it seemed that he liked the idea.

"You won't be hearing from the cops," he lied. He knew that soon everybody in the city would be hearing about Ralinski and his unsigned affidavit.

"Good, good," Major said. "Now finish your drink."

Wright hesitated, then removed his hand from inside his jacket.

Major was back to his jokes again, pouring the booze. Everything was love.

As he sat and drank he thought of Lee Jones. Jones was doing things for the community, and Major was doing things to the community, and had been for years. Both were determined men. There was a lot of fire in Jones's voice, and Major came across with the smooth toughness of a confident pro. He idly wondered if they would ever meet head on, or which faction would eventually win.

CHAPTER

11

He found a restaurant just off the expressway and stopped for something to eat. The place was not crowded. He got a booth in the back and took his time with his ham and eggs.

Just how much of what Major said could he believe? The threat, hell yes, Major was the type of dude to keep his threats. But he could not be concerned with Major's threats, no more than anyone else's, not until it looked like they might be put into action. Major's answer about pushing dope made sense. The penalty for cutting in on someone else seemed to be something Major would have learned well when he was a hit man. So that meant that Lee Jones was wrong in this instance, or that he had done a hell of a snow job. Which left him to wonder why Jones would try to snow him.

Major had denied any connection with the Renegades, which he had expected. So maybe it was not dope, but a connection did exist. Hell, Floyd had hipped him to it first, Ralinski had the affidavit. The connection was there.

It came to him then, through the muddle of everything else. If Major learned that Tom-Tom was spilling to the D.A.'s office, and it was Major who was pulling the strings on the Renegades, then it would be Major who would stand to lose the most. It would have been Major who ordered the hit on Tom-Tom, and because Alicia knew, or maybe was a witness, Major had her hit too.

He suddenly wished he was back in Major's apartment. He would have stopped Wright before he had gotten his hand inside his jacket. He would have taken Major and flung him through the glass wall at the farthest sailboat on the lake. It felt good thinking about it. He could almost see it happening, even though the odds were against him getting away with anything like that.

He ordered another cup of coffee, wishing the hot brew had been a double shot of Grand-Dad. Tank had told Floyd that Tom-Tom was with the gang Sunday night talking them out of showing at the trial Monday. Ralinski had said that Tom-Tom gave his men the slip Friday afternoon, which meant he had no intention of showing for trial. It did not mean Tank was lying about the Sunday meet, but it looked that way.

It seemed to him that no matter how many types of foreign cars they brought into the country, that the VW's still held the market. There was one in practically every block he traveled. He was reminded of how many there were by a battered little green job around the corner from Floyd Hines's shop.

Floyd stuck his head through the curtained archway as he came into the shop. "Hey, Bull," he said, stepping through the curtains. "Didn't expect you'd be in today."

"Well, you said you needed some more bread, didn't you?" he asked, puffing on his cigar. He had lit the cigar partly because he had not had one all day, and partly as a defense against the foulness of Floyd's shop.

"Yeah, man, I can always use more of the green stuff. Say, ah," Floyd pointed at his face, "I thought you got the upper hand in that bash with the Renegades?"

"Different dance," he answered.

Floyd nodded. "Talking about it?"

"No."

"Okay," Floyd shrugged. "I won't either." He was wearing the same T-shirt and jeans he had worn yesterday, they were dirty then, and filthy now. He had skipped shaving, and there was a fuzz upon his dark cheeks. He scratched at the V of a goatee under his lip, his other hand extended palm up. "Now how much did I say that would be?"

"You didn't say, Floyd. And I didn't say I was giving any more." Seeing Floyd, being in this place with its garbage piled high, was beginning to get to him again. Once this was over, he hoped he would never have to deal with the bastard anymore.

Floyd shrugged, blinked. "But ya just said—I mean, last night on the phone ya got a little hot with me. I can understand that. A stud like me has got ta make a buck where he can. But believe me, man. I wouldn't try ta milk my pals. The info cost."

"Sure," he said, handing Floyd another fifty bucks. The information he had gotten so far could only have cost Floyd a couple of beers. But Floyd was the only inside pipeline he had right now, and he had to keep it open.

Floyd stuffed the money into his pocket. "Thanks, man. This'll get us some good information, just wait, ya'll see."

"I'm not going ta wait too long."

Floyd held up a hand. "Hey, man, don't start getting steamed already."

"Then tell me something good. What else have ya come up with?"

"Well, ah," Floyd pulled at his ear, "nothing yet, Bull, just what I tol' ya before."

"Maybe I ought to take my money back now." It was a silly game, but if he did not keep the reins tight on Floyd and dudes like him, he would constantly get screwed.

"Hey, man, don't talk like that. I'll find out what ya want ta know. But it takes a little time. I've still got the Lords ta check. Maybe run down some of Larry Hill's pals."

"Well, get on it, Floyd. The cops ain't giving me much time."

"Yeah, I can dig it, man. Don't worry. Ya don't need nobody else when ya got me working with ya."

"We'll see."

"Let me get ya a beer or somethin'."

"Naw, don't bother."

"No bother, man," Floyd said, darting through the curtained archway. He was back with a couple cans of Bud before the curtains had settled into place.

He took the cold beer from Floyd looking around the place. He could not tell if anything had been rearranged, a junk pile was a junk pile. There were the stacks of newspapers, tires, boxes scattered about, along with a big dose of dust. He popped the tab from the beer, took a swallow. "How the hell can you find anything in this mess?"

"Tell ya a secret, Bull," Floyd said smiling. "Half the time I don't. I've got ta get it all straightened out one of these days. You know it really hampers the legit operation I've got here."

The beer was ice cold just the way he liked it, and it was half gone before he asked, "Know how long Larry Hill's been on the shit?"

"Long time, Bull, long as I've known him."

"What about the others, any of 'em hooked?"

"Naw, just Larry as far as I know. I mean they might smoke a joint or two, but that's about all."

"Have the Renegades been doing any pushing?"

Floyd looked at him somewhat wide eyed, his head cocked to one side as he shrugged. "I don't think so, but I doubt if they would hesitate much if they had the chance." He scratched at his goatee again. "Is that the deal, Bull? Is the whole thing mixed up with dope? If that's it, then I've been looking at things from the wrong angle. I've got some contacts that I—"

"I don't know if that's it or not, Floyd. But it is something to look at."

Floyd took a swallow of his beer, wiping his mouth with the back of his hand. "Yeah, man, yeah. I'll get on it right away."

"You do that. I'll check with you later tonight."

Vern lived in a section on the far South side known as LaLina Park. It was a nice quiet community full of grass and trees. There were some new homes, but the bulk were thirty-or forty-year-old brick jobs like the one Vern owned. Three years ago, when Vern was looking for a place to buy, the neighborhood had been primarily white. But in the four months it took for the papers to go through and for him to move, there were only six white families left in the whole of LaLina Park.

The front of Vern's place was mostly a picture window overlooking shrubs, and a long richly green lawn, bathing in the warm late afternoon sun.

He parked on the side drive leading to the two-car garage. The smells of newly cut grass and fresh paint were in the air. He could never come out here without wondering if someday he would do the family scene himself. Yet it was difficult for him to picture himself cutting grass, attending block club meetings, and all the other crap that goes along with owning a home.

He only rang the door bell once, and Marge was there with smiles to greet him. She was a tiny little thing, as black as ink, and better looking than a stack of fifties. She wore a blue denim shift with matching scarf that bundled her thick Afro. "Bull," she said, her brown eyes clear and bright. She wore no make-up, her long lashes were her own. There was something pure about her. If he envied Vern anything, he envied him Marge.

"How ya doing, doll?" he said, bending down and hugging her.

"Fine, Bull, just fine. I can't say you're looking that well."

"Would ya believe I fell down the stairs?"

She nodded. "If you say so. Say, when are you coming by for dinner? You're always calling, but its been a long time since you've sat with us."

"Yeah," he admitted, "it has. But you know me, Marge. Guess I'm afraid I might get used to it, and then what? Vern's my pal. I don't want to go breaking up his home."

She laughed. "You're still full of it, aren't you?"

He laughed with her. "Well, you know. Is Vern asleep?"

"Surprisingly no. He came in this morning all pepped up. He's mowed the lawn, fixed the lock on the back fence and even painted it. Right now he's down in the work shop, trying to fix a toaster I've been after him to look at for a month."

"Hey, what have ya been feeding him?"

She put a finger to her lips. "Not so loud. He doesn't know it yet, but I found this little shop back in the old neighborhood—" She started laughing again before she had finished.

Vern's work shop was in the back part of the basement next to the utility room. He had completed the paneling of the front part of the basement just last summer. It was a good job, too, with dark oak walls, indirect lighting, even a wet bar. They had had a hell of a New Year's Eve party down here—he had had a hangover for a week.

Vern turned from his work-bench as he came in. "Just in time. Bull, come here and hold this."

Pegboard covered the walls of the little room, with hammer, saws, and other tools hanging from them. Vern had the toaster upside-down on the work-bench, its bottom off and a couple of screws and parts lying nearby.

"Hold what?" he asked.

"That little part right there," Vern said, pointing to a metal brace inside the toaster.

He got a screwdriver, holding the piece down while Vern worked on it with another screwdriver. There was the sound of metal against metal and when Vern brought his screwdriver up, a spring was wrapped around it.

Vern nodded. "Okay, Bull, you can stop holding it now, and just because you're my friend, I won't tell Marge you broke her toaster."

"Oh, thanks," he laughed at him.

Vern asked about his swollen jaw and he told him. He told him everything he had not had time to tell him before, about Floyd, what went on at the Renegades' headquarters, his visit from Sharon

Woods. He even told him about Lee Jones and the call he had paid Sammy Major. They were interrupted only once, when Marge brought them tall glasses of iced tea. By the time he had finished, the tea was gone, Vern was working on his second cigarette, and he was half through with a cigar.

"Well," Vern said. "These last couple of days have been active."

"Have you had chance to read the affidavit Ralinski got from Green?"

"I've skimmed through it, why?"

"This dope angle is what I'm wondering about. I don't know why I can't shake it."

"Green didn't mention it," Vern said. "They were doing a lot of things, though, getting protection money from the store owners in the neighborhood, a few armed robberies, some burglaries. Most anything else, but no dope."

"Maybe it's their next step."

"It could be," Vern agreed with a nod. "Major has got a lot of manpower in the Renegades. He could be planning a take-over."

He had not thought of it, but why not? With the army the Renegades would provide for Major, he could take just about whatever he wanted from the syndicate and hold it.

"Did ya ever get any word from the Roosevelt Street Precinct?"

"Yeah," Vern said, taking a last drag on his cigarette before putting it out. "They found some spent .38 shells, and were able to retrieve some of the slugs out of the wall and floor. The slugs were pretty beat up, I don't know if they will help. I haven't heard from ballistics, but I'm betting they match the shells we picked up around that phone booth."

If true, it would mean the same dude that got Alicia had tried to get him. Or at least that the same gun had been used. "It's beginning to fall in line."

"Slowly," Vern said.

"How much sweat is Hamilton causing you?"

"Not as much as you. Don't worry, I'm used to him."

The phone rang, its shrill could be heard loud and clear from the extension by the basement stairs.

"Ten to five it's for me," Vern said.

"No thanks, the odds aren't good enough for me."

It was only a moment before Marge called down, and Vern went to the phone.

"Feel like dropping me off?" Vern asked, on his return. There was something light about his expression, a slackness, a relief.

"Sure, where to?"

"Riter Avenue. Looks like we finally get the chance to unwrap Ralinski's affidavit."

"What's up?"

"Well, number one, ballistics matched those shells."

"And number two?"

"They've found Tom-Tom Green."

"Is there a number three?"

Vern nodded. "Green's dead."

CHAPTER

12

Vern told him the rest of
the story on the way to Riter Avenue. After finding
the spent shells and slugs, the Roosevelt Street
Precinct conducted a routine inquiry, checking
with the neighbors to see if they had noticed anyone hanging around the building. They turned up
an old lady who said she heard something like fire-
crackers last Friday night coming from another
condemned building, on the other side of the vacant lot from the one Bull had been in. They
checked the building, and found Green in a second-
floor apartment with two holes in his chest.

"He's been dead since Friday, huh?"

126

"That's the way it looks, Bull. He slipped away from Ralinski's men Friday afternoon, and got hit Friday night."

"Alicia went into hiding Friday night."

"Yeah, seems like it's adding up the way we had it figured."

He thought for a moment. "It also means that Tank lied to Floyd about that Sunday meet. I can understand him lying to the cops, but why to Floyd, why even mention Green at all."

"We'll be getting the answers soon, Bull. There's pick-up orders out for the Renegades, Wright, and Major."

"Some party you dudes are throwing."

"Yeah, ain't it though."

When he got to Riter Avenue, he had to park on the corner because he could not get farther down the block. The street was cluttered with an assortment of police cars, both blue and white squadrols, and unmarked jobs. The meat wagon was there to get the body, and there were more people milling around than there probably were during the riot. Kids playing tag, men young and old, from suits to shirt sleeves, women with their hair in rollers and housecoats, all crushed together in the hot afternoon sun. The windows were full too, black faces massed there, staring out. It reminded him of Monday night, when he had come to, and the people cramming to see what had happened. The spectacle of death! How the crowds loved it.

He followed Vern as he pushed his way through the crowd to the corridor of uniformed cops that were holding them back. Vern flashed his badge, and they were let through to the group that was standing by the meat wagon. Hamilton was there, his tie loose about his neck, his bald head wet with sweat. Charlie, Wes, and Ralinski were there too, along with a couple of white dudes he had not seen before, but they had the look of cops, the square build, the hard faces.

"What's he doing here?" Hamilton asked, mopping his forehead with his handkerchief.

"He was with me when Charlie called," Vern answered.

Here we go again, he thought. "If you want me to split, I'll cut right now."

"That's—" Hamilton started.

"That won't be necessary, Mr. Benson," Ralinski said. He was wearing a light tan double-breasted number complete with vest, and he looked more comfortable than anyone else around. "We can't rightly exclude Mr. Benson from what we've found, Lieutenant. He's got a lot of interest in this case."

"I believe that," Hamilton said frowning.

Wes smiled, winking at him through his horn-rimmed glasses.

At last he had someone in his corner who pulled more weight than Hamilton. It was a strange feeling, but a good one.

"Has positive identification been made?" Vern asked.

"I took care of that," Ralinski said. "It's Green."

"Yeah, and we got a bonus," Charlie said with a nod. "Larry Hill was in there too. He caught one in the head. They've both been dead for some time, we're guessing three or four days, probably since Friday."

At least it meant it was not Larry Hill who had called him last night, or Tom-Tom Green for that matter. "How was Hill's arms?" he asked.

Hamilton glared at him. "I'll tolerate you being here, Benson, but you keep your trap shut."

"He had more holes in his arms than a precinct's bulletin board," Ralinski said. "Had you heard he was a junkie?"

"Yeah, but this was the first time it's been proven."

"Ralinski, I think you're superseding your authority."

"On the contrary, Lieutenant. Check your statute books. This has been the D.A.'s case all along. But I don't think we need to be squabbling amongst ourselves in front of the press."

Wes looked up from the pad he had been writing in. "Okay, fellows," he said, pushing his glasses back onto his nose. He stuck the pad and pen in his pocket, held his hands up. "I'll only print what you tell me."

"Mr. Westerfield, I think it would be better if you wait in your car," Ralinski said. "I'll get back to you before I leave."

Wes looked back and forth from Ralinski to Hamilton, shrugged. "Okay, Mr. Ralinski, I'll be waiting."

"How'd it look?" Vern asked, after Wes had gone.

"The bodies were found in separate rooms," Charlie said. "We only located one gun, .38 snub nose that was in Hill's hand. Two chambers were fired. They could've blasted each other, but it wouldn't explain the separate rooms or the missing gun. Hill didn't do any running around after he caught that slug in the head, and it looks like Green dropped where he was hit too."

"So we're looking for a third party," Vern said.

"Alicia," he said, almost to himself, not quite knowing why. Instead of becoming clearer, things were getting more confused.

Vern looked around at him. "Alicia's a possibility."

He did not want to believe it. Alicia had killed her own brother, was that what she was running from? If Larry had killed Green, did she love Green so much that she would kill her brother in revenge? "If we tie it up that way," he said, "that still leaves our friend with the .38 automatic."

"Yes, we mustn't forget about him." Hamilton said, looking directly at him, accusing him with a stare.

"For the record, Lieutenant," Ralinski said, his voice raised, "the D.A.'s office is presuming Mr. Benson has been telling the truth. I hope there will be no need for me to clarify my position."

Hamilton's thick lips stretched wide in his frown. "All right, Ralinski, don't listen to me, let him con you. You'll learn." He paused long enough to glare at him again, then turned back to Ralinski. "If you want me, I'll be back at the precinct."

Hamilton walked off with Charlie, the two white cops following them.

"Well, thanks for taking up for me."

"It's not accepted," Ralinski said. "That was a very informative talk we had yesterday. I had a chance to analyze myself." He nodded. "I believe your story, Mr. Benson. Maybe the lieutenant is right, maybe you are conning me. But I do know he was going about it the wrong way. And I know that if you are lying, I'll find out. Now, if you'll excuse me. I have to see Mr. Westerfield before I get back to my office."

"Is he for me or against me?" he asked Vern, as he watched Ralinski disappear into the crowd.

"Hell," Vern said, rubbing his long chin. "Flip a coin."

With the cops out rounding up the Renegades and Major, there was not much for him to do but go back to the hotel and wait. Giving Floyd that extra fifty was proving to be a waste now. Hell, with the bodies, and Ralinski's affidavit, the Renegades were in for a rough quiz. Somebody would crack, and they would probably have the whole thing cleaned up by supper.

Sam Devlin and Ed Lambert were at the end of the bar playing cards when he came into the lounge. Sam was behind the bar, and Ed was overlapping a stool. The ball game was on TV, but Sam had the volume down so low you would just about have to sit on top of the damn thing to learn what was going on. There was a dude in work overalls sitting at the bar across from the set, and a couple in one of the side booths. If not for them, the place would have been empty. It would fill again in an hour or so as the people got off from work.

"The more he keeps tellin' me he's lost his

touch, the more this ol' bastard beats me," Ed said, slicking his process back with his open hand.

"Go easy on him, Sam, we don't want to lose the best cook on the South side."

"Lose'em, hell," Sam cracked in his raspy voice. "When I'm finished wit'em, he'll be workin' fa nutten."

They were playing with chips, and they usually ran it at a buck a chip. A quick count and he saw that there was ten dollars riding in the pot.

"How many cards, Ed, or do ya want ta call it quits right now," Sam smiled at him.

He glanced over Ed's beefy shoulder. He was holding two pair, jacks and sixes with a deuce kicker. Ed discarded the deuce. "Just one big one, Sam, and make it good."

"I'll do what I can fa ya, Ed," Sam said, passing him his card. "Dealer takes two."

Ed stuck the card in with his others, shuffled them about, then cuffed them in his hand before taking a look at them. Sam had dealt him another six.

"Hey, now, Ed," Sam said. "Is that a smile on that ugly mug of yo'ns?"

"Tell ya what, old man," Ed said, tossing some chips onto the pile. "That's going to cost you five more, ta see if I'm fooling."

"My, my, my. On the strength of one card, too. Bull, looks like ya've brought Ed here some luck. Well, Ed, seein' as how generous ya've been ta me, I'm gonna see if'n I can do the same fa ya. Here's yar five, and back ya another five."

He could smell the come-on for miles. There

was a sparkle in Sam's eyes. Ed did not have too many ways to go, if he got up now he was certainly the loser. Of course Sam could have been trying to buy the hand.

Ed sighed. "Damn you, Sam. I'll see it. What have ya got?"

Sam shrugged his bony shoulders. "Little ol' full house, Ed, that's all," Sam said, displaying his cards. "Nines over fours."

"See what I mean?" Ed said, throwing his cards down. "Every goddamn time."

"You're welcome ta another hand," Sam laughed at him.

"Not me. I'm going back to the kitchen where it's safe. The worse that can happen back there is the stove blows up on me."

They all laughed at that, even Ed, his big gut jiggling.

"How 'bout ya, Bull?" Sam asked. "Maybe I can win this place from ya."

"Naw, Sam, I learned long ago not ta mess with the master." It was more to the compliment than just the words. They both knew that Sam was all right for the little fun sets, but that he did not have it anymore to hang in with the long-haul, pressure games.

Sam winked at him. "Thanks, Bull."

"Want me ta whip you up anything?" Ed asked, on his way to the kitchen.

"I had a late breakfast," he answered.

"A drink then?" Sam asked.

"There's a good idea."

Sam pushed the cards and chips out of the way

133

when he came back with the double Grand-Dad. "That chick gettin' killed beginning ta get ya down?" Sam asked, after he had taken the first soothing swallow of his drink.

"Not anymore," he said, and he told Sam about the cops rounding up the Renegades and Major.

"Well, Vern'll handle it from now on," Sam said. "Ya ain't got nothing ta worry 'bout."

"Yeah," he said, and then realized that was not the way he wanted it. He wanted to be right in there, taking care of the bastard who killed Alicia, not sitting here watching the ice melt in his drink. But what else could he do?

He tried watching part of the ball game, but it could not hold his interest. He went back to his office and worked on the invoices, but he could not really concentrate on that either. He wound up dusting and straightening tables, and helping Sam behind the bar.

It was getting close to five, and the lounge was beginning to fill up. The TV was off, quarters were being dropped into the juke box. Sly had come up with a new one, and the sound of drums, bass, and electric piano was bouncing off the walls.

Sam was working the back half of the bar, and he was handling the front, when Sid McFadden came in. Although McFadden was in the lounge two, maybe three times a week, he never made it twice in a row, or this early.

McFadden got a stool in the corner of his half of the bar, away from everybody else.

"How're you doing, Mr. McFadden. What'll it be?"

"Beer'll be fine," McFadden said wiping his hands with his handkerchief. "It's been pretty warm today. The air conditioner broke down in the shop."

"Yeah, that can be rough," he said, drawing the beer and bringing it to him.

McFadden began sipping his beer, and he turned away.

"Oh, Bull."

"Yeah, Mr. McFadden?"

McFadden wiped his face with his hand, scratched his oversized nose. "Ah—"

"Yeah?"

"It's, it's good beer," McFadden said, nodding.

"We try to keep the best on tap." He turned away again.

"Oh, Bull."

What the hell was he going to be, a yo-yo? "Is there something bothering you, Mr. McFadden?"

"Well, ah," McFadden wiped his face again, looked around the place, sweat was showing all along his recessed hairline. He took another sip of his beer, leaned forward, and beckoned him to come closer.

He did not really want to hear what McFadden had to say. After all this time, after being cool with it, McFadden was now getting ready to proposition him.

"Now look, Mr. McFadden—" he started.

"It's about Monday night," McFadden said. "The night of the shooting. I saw the man who did it."

"**R**un that by me again."
The volume of the juke box was not that high. He
should not have had any trouble hearing McFadden. Wishful thinking, dreaming, what could he
credit it to? Was he so desperate to find something
to throw him back into things?

"I saw the man who did it," McFadden re-
peated.

No mistakes this time. He heard him plainly. He
felt his heart beat faster inside his chest. It had not
been two full days since Alicia was blown away,
but a lot had gone down. There had been a lot of
name calling, swinging fists, and a bullet or two

that came close to having his old lady cash in his insurance policy. There had been a lot of heavy thinking and pushing for the right answers, for something to put it all together. Now up popped McFadden, a little late since the cops were busting things open, but welcome all the same. "Information like that should be given to the cops," he said, feeling that was what the situation called for, and knowing what McFadden's answer would be.

"You were the one who got shot at, Bull, and besides, I—I get kind of nervous when I talk to the police."

"Yeah, okay," he said. With McFadden not willing to talk to the cops, the best he could do was take the information and turn it over to Vern. An eye witness is always best, yet with the Renegades and Major already being quizzed, the information would help Vern just as well. "Lay it on me, Mr. McFadden, what'd ya see?"

McFadden looked down at his beer, took a sip of it, licked his lips. "I was in the next block over," he said with a nod. "On Yarby, right across from the alley in the doorway of that old red brick building." He looked down at his beer again, maybe expecting to be asked what he was doing standing in a doorway that late at night. "I heard the shooting, then this man comes running up to the mouth of the alley with a gun in his hand. He stopped, stuck the gun in his belt, then walked out onto the street, got in a car, and drove off."

"What'd he look like?"

McFadden shrugged. "He wasn't too big. He was wearing black trousers and a black jacket. He hadn't shaved for a while, and his hair was kind of messed up."

That was the bastard all right, the dude who had been sleeping in his lounge, or pretending to be! "Were you able to get the car license?"

"No. But it was a Volkswagon, in pretty bad shape too. It was dark, but not black, maybe blue or brown."

"Could it have been dark green?" He thought of the dark green VW he had seen both yesterday and today, once in front of the Renegades headquarters, and once around the corner from Floyd's.

"Yes," McFadden said nodding. "That's possible. Why, do you know the car?"

"Maybe," he said, thanking McFadden, telling him he had a free bar tab there whenever he wanted, and went back to his office. He phoned the Moore Street Precinct, but Vern was not there. He was downtown at the central station where the Renegades and Major had been taken for questioning under the directions of the D.A.'s office. It took him a good ten minutes waiting on the line to central, before Vern came to the phone.

"How's it going?" he asked.

"Not as fast as we'd expected," Vern said. "But we'll wear 'em down."

"Who's there?"

"Well, Major and Wright split a little over an hour ago. Money and a big time lawyer will do that for you. But we're not worried. All we've got to do is get one of the Renegades to go along with Green's affidavit, then we can pull Wright back in here, and sweat him until he implicates Major. It's not going to be that rough. The Renegades aren't as hard as they think they are."

"Which ones have you got?"

"What's left of the brains, Dex, Bo, Tank. Why?"

"Just wondering," he lied.

"Hey, Bull, come on. There's something else to this call."

Vern knew him too well. "Yeah, there is," he said. "Hang close to the phone, I'll be getting back to you."

"Now, wait a minute, Bull—" He heard Vern shout through the receiver as he hung up.

He expected the receiver to jump right out of its cradle in Vern's return call, but it did not. Maybe Vern was going to wait and see what turned. Or perhaps it was like Sharon Woods suggested, that the cops were watching the lounge, and Vern had called and alerted them.

He got his bottle of Grand-Dad out of the bottom drawer, poured himself a double and knocked it right down. The .38 was lying in the same drawer. He picked it up, feeling the cool comfort of its blue steel in his hand. It had helped him last night. Without it he would not have been around today. He looked at the .38 for a moment, the way the light reflected off its blunt barrel, the dull copper-colored slugs in the chambers, then he put it back in the drawer. If he was figuring things right, the .38 was just too impersonal a weapon.

He got caught in the rush hour traffic on the Tri-City expressway heading for the West side. He cursed and honked his way to the nearest down-town exit ramp, and darted back and forth between through and side streets.

He did not see the VW around the corner from Floyd Hines's shop as he had earlier today. There were a couple of others about, a light blue van with "Smith and Sons TV Repair" stenciled on its side and a highly polished little yellow number that looked factory new. But there was no signs of the dark green battered job that he was inter-ested in.

The street was filled, kids playing, men and women coming home after doing their eight hours for the man, some just leaving for work. He did not notice any movement inside Floyd's shop as he drove by, only a bright red "closed" sign on the door. Damnit, he had missed them.

A car horn honked behind him. He checked his rear view mirror and saw an old lady shaking a finger at him. He had not realized it, but seeing the "closed" sign, he had stopped in the middle of the street and was staring at the damn thing. He waved to the old bag, started up again and drove to the mouth of the alley. Maybe he would be able to get into the shop from the back. Maybe there would be something there to indicate where they had gone.

He pulled the Caddy into the narrow alley. There, hugged close to the building among the row of garbage cans and fire escapes, sat the green VW. He got out of his car, going the rest of the way on foot at a casual pace. A dirty gray tom cat perched atop a lidless garbage can, eyed him challengingly, his hair standing straight along the ridge of his back. At the other end of the alley some kids were playing handball, their laughter reaching him, somehow pointing out the seriousness of his position.

He had not been sure until he had gotten closer to the VW, but yes, it was the same one he had seen Marv Fellows leaning against in front of the Renegades headquarters. Its back seat was heavy with boxes and ledger books. He had gotten here just in time.

Like the front of Floyd's shop, the stairs to the back door were recessed. The one window was barred and covered over, preventing him from seeing inside. He leaned close to the door, hoping to hear them, to get an idea where they were.

The door swung open suddenly, with Marv standing there grinning, pointing an automatic at his face. "Say, big man, nice of ya to come by and see us off."

"That wasn't quite my idea," he said, the dark eye of the automatic staring at him.

"Come on, nice and easy," Marv said, motioning with the gun. "Inside."

He was sure to get it in the back if he tried to run. If he was going to go, he was going to go with his hands around Marv's neck.

He looked around as the door was closed behind him. Floyd was leaning against it, a long barrel revolver in his hand. He was cleaner now, wearing a pair of brown bells, with a darker brown nylon jacket. "I was wondering how long it would take ya to put it together, Bull."

"It took some help," he said.

"Yeah, well ya didn't bring it with ya," Marv said. "We saw ya pass by up front."

The back room seemed as junky, if not worse off, than the front part of the shop. Boxes were piled everywhere. The only clear area was to the left of the door where they were standing. There was a desk just a few feet away, directly across from the curtained archway leading up front. He was directed to stand by the desk with his hands behind his head, and face the wall while Marv patted him down.

"He's clean," Marv said.

"Ya can turn around, Bull, but keep those hands up."

They stood about six feet away from him, one on either side, looking like twins, except that Marv's bells and jacket were in blue. Yesterday, Marv had been close-shaven, his Afro high. Today, the Afro was glossier, not quite as tall, and there were traces of a mustache and sideburns. And as on Monday night, Marv was not wearing the ruby earring. The dark puncture of the pierced ear showed clearly against his light complexion. Hell, Marv was the triggerman all right, the VW and the automatic told him that. He had even felt a twinge of recognition when he saw Marv in front of the Renegades headquarters yesterday. Then he had not been sure, but the situation along with the mustache and sideburns helped him.

"When did ya recognize Marv?" Floyd asked.

"Just now, actually."

Marv grinned widely, and Floyd nodded, saying, "That dude grows hair like his old man was Wolfman or somebody. Hell, he could have a full beard twice a week if he wanted."

Then suddenly he knew Floyd was back of the whole thing. "It's you, ain't it, Floyd? I mean Sammy Major doesn't know a damn thing about this deal?" Things being the way they were, he certainly had nothing to lose by asking the question.

"Hey, now, man. That's fancy, really fancy," Floyd said. "Ya got all of that. Huh?"

It was not fancy thinking. It was the only way things made sense. He had worked out part of it on his way over here, and the rest was beginning to fall in line. Major had told him the truth. Major wanted nothing to do with punks like the Renegades. But Floyd's existence depended on them. And if the main point of Green's affidavit was true, the involvement of Windy Wright, it meant that Wright and Floyd were in it together.

"How long have you known Wright?" he asked.

Floyd's grin went away, then came back even stronger. He shrugged. "Since reform school, Bull. You know it all, then?"

"No, not all," he said, but it was coming easy now the more he thought about it. The main thing though was to keep Floyd talking. He did not believe they were planning to take him with them. There was enough fire power in either of their guns to stop him with one slug. He could only hope that when the time came, he could move fast enough and get at least one of them.

"Well, let me 'plain a few things to ya, Bull," Floyd said.

"Don't explain shit to him," Marv said. "We won, he lost, that's enough."

"Naw, that's no good, Marv. Relax. I've known Bull for a long while. He deserves some answers."

"You and Wright had a sweet thing, Floyd, using Major's name as a front. I'm betting it was your idea."

"I'll take the credit," Floyd said, rubbing his goatee. "And sweet it was, man. Two more months, Bull, that's all, just two, and we would have had the West side. I'm not just talking about walking bad out in the street. Man, I'm talking about owning it. Everything from numbers to drugs, it would have been ours. We would have taken it from the big cats and kept it."

"Then Green blows the whole deal with his affidavit," he said, measuring the steps it would take to reach them, deciding on which one to go after.

"Yeah, man, ain't that a trip? See, none of the Renegades knew about the big take-over plans, or that I was running the whole deal, 'cept Marv and Larry. Hell, they've been working for me from the get."

Floyd had had things laid out well. With Marv and Larry keeping tabs on the Renegades, and Wright doing the same to Major, Floyd had been able to develop his plans smoothly.

"Tom-Tom started having second thoughts about the affidavit and all." Floyd continued. "He came to me as an old pal to get money to split the city."

"He told you about the affidavit and you knew you'd have to ice him for good. So you set him up for Larry and Marv to take care of him."

144

"That's right, Bull," Floyd said. "Only they had a complication."

"Yeah, I can imagine. Alicia was there." He wished he had brought the gun, then, wished he had bust through the door blasting.

"They must have been planning to leave town together. I should have figured it. Well, anyway Larry took care of Tom-Tom, but he didn't have the balls to ice his own sister, and he held Marv back long enough for her to get away."

"But nobody holds Marv for very long," he said. His arms were beginning to get tired. It would certainly slow him down if he did not make his move soon.

"The bastard took his eyes off me for a second," Marv said. "One goddamn second and I had him."

"It's nice to see someone who enjoys his job."

"I do, big man," Marv said, waving the automatic. "I do."

"And he's dedicated," Floyd said. "He got close enough to Alicia to tail her to your neighborhood where she gave him the slip. But he kept looking, man. Three goddamn days he kept looking, until he saw her going into your lounge Monday night. He had a beard by then, different clothes, she didn't know him that well anyway, and she didn't recognize him when he went in your place." Floyd shrugged. "Hell, if she had, he would've blasted her right there instead of waiting for her to come out."

"And when you called me yesterday?" He began slowly to shift his weight to one foot, readying himself to spring forward.

145

"I thought that was pretty cute," Floyd said. "That call was just a way to locate ya, so Marv could call ya back and say he was Larry. Most of what I told ya was shit anyway, 'cept Larry being a hop-head. Hell, I hooked him. He did everything I told him, up 'til Friday." Floyd paused, his body heaved in a deep sigh. He was not grinning anymore. "Hope I've answered all your questions, Bull. Marv—"

Marv stepped forward raising the automatic. "Say good-bye, big man."

He could feel the sweat running down his back. Marv was the closest now, and Marv was the one he would have to go for. A fake to his right, and then he would try, low and fast.

"You'd better say good-bye, too, punk."

Everything seemed to freeze. The voice had come from the curtained archway. Sammy Major stood there, flanked on each side by the two dudes he had seen at Major's apartment earlier. All three were holding guns, cool and steady in their readiness.

"Windy and me just finished a little talk," Major said. His eyes were narrow, the lips in a frown. "You know, he actually tol' me he was sorry. It was the last thing he said."

Marv's grin got wider, and he winked at him, as if to say, watch this shit, big man, and he spun and fired. Major moaned, clutching his chest.

He jumped over and behind the desk, as the room erupted in gun fire. There were more groans, curses, and slugs ricocheting. He could not see what was going on. From behind the desk he could see only the back door. In these close quarters the fight would not last long, and whoever won would certainly come after him.

Floyd was there, his back to the door firing. A slug shattered the window, chipped the door near Floyd's head. Then Floyd had the door open, and was out onto the alley.

He got hold of the desk, braced his foot against the wall and pushed out. He heard the slugs embed themselves into the desk, strike the floor near him. But he got the desk between him and the door, and then he was out.

The VW was still there. Maybe Marv had the keys. Floyd was down at the other end of the alley. Floyd leapt onto a garbage can, reached the fire escape of the corner building and began climbing. The kids were not playing handball anymore, they were gone. He did not even see any cars pass the mouth of the alley. The sound of gun fire, and anyone with any sense takes cover. The crowds would not come out until later, when it was quiet and safe.

He used the same garbage can Floyd had used. Just as he got his first foot hold on the fire escape, a slug nicked at the ladder above his head. Marv staggered forward in the alley, his shirt and jacket covered with blood, the automatic weaving in his hand. He coughed and blood spurted from his mouth. His gun fell to the pavement as he grabbed his throat, coughed again, and pitched forward.

He did not take the time to reflect whether Major

147

and his hoods were in any shape to come after him, he just swung back and continued up the ladder. Floyd was already over the top.

The roofs of the buildings were just as coated with debris as the alley. Peering from the fire escape, eye-level with the roof, he could see the bottles, beer cans, and trash scattered about the TV antennas, chimneys, skylights, and little huts that were the roof entrances to the buildings. But no Floyd. The buildings were so close together, Floyd could be down at the other end by now.

He stood on the roof in a crouch, ready to move in an instant. The roofs were nearly carbon copies in design. Each had a huge brick chimney standing over six feet tall on the right-hand side of the building. Across from the chimney, and a little to the front was the entrance to the building. On the other side of the huts lay the oblong skylights, their glass broken and patched.

He started for the first entrance slowly. Floyd could be there waiting, or behind the chimney, or in the building, or halfway to China. The late day sun was at his back, and his shadow slid along the roof before him. It had been hot all day, and yet he felt like he was caught in a snow storm.

He was three feet away from the entrance when Floyd stepped out from behind the hut and fired. He never heard a gun sound as loud, the flame rushing from the long barrel. Floyd's eyes were wide, with a wild, frightened look on his sweaty face. Bull Benson, you're a dumb son-of-a-bitch, he told himself, as the slug tore into his left arm knocking him back hard against the chimney.

Floyd took aim this time, slow, sure.

There was no feeling in his left arm, only an icy tingle in his finger tips. The dead weight of the arm kept him off balance.

Floyd squeezed the trigger, and the hammer fell on an empty chamber. He mumbled something to himself, the corner of his mouth curling, and he tried again, another empty chamber and another.

"What's the matter, Floyd," he laughed at him. "Can't ya handle a simple hit?"

"Shit," Floyd shouted, and threw the revolver at him.

He ducked as the gun smashed into the chimney, and by the time he righted himself, Floyd was almost on top of him, a long blade knife in his hand.

He pushed off from the chimney towards the back of the roof, and Floyd missed with the first pass of the knife. Floyd swung back around, and came for him, panting, the red glow of the sun bouncing off the shiny blade.

"I'm gonna carve your ass so thin the rats'll be eating off of ya for a month."

Floyd had handled a knife before. There was confidence in his stance, the low crouch, the knife extended, slowly slicing the air before him. He tried moving to his right, but Floyd was there quicker. He moved to his left and it was the same thing. If he kept backing up he would wind up in the alley.

He kicked out at Floyd, and the knife was there, ripping his pants leg, slashing his ankle. Floyd was smiling again, and he did not appear to be sweating as much as before. There were plenty of bottles around. If only he could get hold of one.

He stepped back onto something, stumbled, almost fell, and Floyd came in fast. The blade dug in across his chest, along the upper part of his thigh, ripped at his numb arm. He caught Floyd's wrist as the blade was inches from his throat.

It was a contest of strength, Floyd bearing down with both hands, and him holding the blade off. It was a contest Floyd would not win, could not win. The blade quivered before his face. Neither spoke. There were only the sounds of their groans, the shuffling of their feet.

He bent Floyd's hands back slightly, a little more, then he brought his knee up hard. Floyd cried out as the knee smashed into his balls. The knife fell to the roof. He flung Floyd back, away from the knife, and rushed in on him. He chopped down, his fist striking against the side of Floyd's face, feeling jaw bones crack beneath the flesh. Then a backhanded upper-cut sent Floyd tumbling towards the edge of the roof.

He was there, reaching out, grabbing the nylon jacket as Floyd went over. Floyd's weight almost pulled him off the roof too. He lay there, his arm hanging over the side, a firm grip about the collar of the jacket. Floyd looked up at him, clawing at the building, his jaw hanging at an awkward angle, blood at both corners of his mouth. Floyd was trying to talk, but only garbled noises were coming out. The jacket was strong. It would hold. He might be able to get him back onto the roof.

He looked down at Floyd, breathing deeply, trying to muster enough strength to pull him back up. But it was not Floyd's face there anymore, it was not Floyd's eyes pleading with him. It was Alicia. Alicia lying on the sidewalk, bloody and still. Alicia who had got hooked up with the wrong people and paid for it.

"What the fuck for?" he said, and he let go.

Floyd was still clawing at the building as he fell, grabbing handfuls of air in a vain attempt to save himself. He landed head first with a solid smack, bounced once, and settled in a tangled crimson heap.

He rolled away from the edge, got to a sitting position, and dug a cigar out of his pocket. It was done now. He had kept his promise to Alicia. He tore the cigar wrapper off with his teeth, lit up, and took two deep drags. Hamilton would be off his back too, there were enough bodies and evidence around to satisfy him. He got to his feet. The numbness was beginning to leave his arm, a steady throb taking its place. As he started for the fire escape, he heard the wail of police sirens, and he saw that the setting sun had turned the sky a dusky red.